Christine Piff has appeared on Channel Four's
Twenty/Twenty Vision, BBC's Russell Harty
Show and other television and radio
programmes. As a result of the huge response
she received, she has now launched a support
link for the facially handicapped, also called
Let's Face It, to enable them to share their
experiences and to pass on advice on ways of
dealing with their problems.

Let's Face It

CHRISTINE PIFF

SPHERE BOOKS LIMITED

First published in Great Britain by
Victor Gollancz Ltd 1985
Copyright © Christine Piff 1985
Published by Sphere Books Ltd 1986
27 Wright's Lane, London W8 5SW
Reprinted 1986 (twice)

Printed and bound in Great Britain by
Cox & Wyman Ltd, Reading

Let's Face It

Chapter One

It was the biggest, hardest most squeezable kiss I had ever had! So passionate was it that I tumbled helplessly to the floor. What a vulnerable place to be, flat on my back and fighting off so many amorous advances. 'Let me.' 'Let me.' 'It's my turn.' 'Poor Auntie Chris, I'll pull you up!'

I can't recall exactly what caused this scene, but then it was quite normal for me to take on sixteen under-fives in such a playful manner. Yet I know it was only about a week later that I first became aware that my face was slightly tender where I had received my lovely kisses.

December 1976 was a busy and exciting time of year for me. We were beginning to think of Christmas and our concerts, so there was lots of planning to be done. And on Tuesdays I was helping with my younger son's football lessons. I hesitate to call them lessons. I assisted a very athletic youth from Wellington College to try to control some thirty seven-year-olds. Boy, was it fun! It took me a while to realise that these angels in football boots had boundless energy.

It was freezing cold that particular Tuesday morning and I wasn't too sure if the teachers would let the boys out as the field was covered in frost. Out they came, as keen as mustard, some in tracksuits and others too eager to change. We ran around the pitch with me up among the goodies, doing me the world of good, I thought. Suddenly my face became so agonisingly uncomfortable I had to stop. This was the first time that I thought something was wrong.

Like most women, I was far too busy to do anything sensible like visiting the doctor. Had it been my husband or one of the children, a different matter. After all—it was just a bruise.

I suppose I should tell you a little about myself to put you in the picture. I was then thirty-five years old and had been blissfully happily married to my husband Chris for fourteen years. We had three children, Claire eleven, Matthew nine, and Dominic seven, had lived in Crowthorne, Berkshire, for ten years and were very, very happy. My whole life, it seemed, revolved around children, for as a qualified Nursery Nurse I also spent every morning at a local play school. This didn't interfere with my husband or my children and it satisfied a need in me to be with the people I like best: children. Apart from the football, I also helped in my elder son's school pottery class. I suppose I happened to be there when they asked. I have never laughed so much. The boys were ten and eleven years old, the top of the school and frightfully grown up. But all you had to do was drop a few football scores, name a few motor bikes, and you were in! The friendship with these boys was priceless, and even today as I see them coming out of their senior school—even if they don't speak to me—there's a look that says 'I remember'.

Now when I look back at Christmases I always say, 'That was the happiest one of all.' Truly 1976 was a super Christmas. We spent Boxing Day with very close friends of ours, their parents and children—I suppose in all there were fifteen of us. The day was geared to laughter from beginning to end. But my face was now a constant pain and when I bent forward the pressure in my head was unbearable. By now, Chris was aware of my discomfort and dragged me to the doctor the following day. Erysipelas was the diagnosis and I was put on a course of antibiotics and had an appointment for the following week.

Feeling happier for visiting the doctor, I made plans for the New Year. We had tickets for the first time for the Parent-Teacher Association Ball at Wellington College. Six of us were going and I was really looking forward to it. One week, one new evening dress and nearly a week's supply of antibiotics later came the Ball. It was freezing! Pale blue chiffon does your morale the world of good, but nothing underneath keeps warm.

I should have worn long johns. 'Brandy and champagne—well, Babycham—that's the answer,' said Sue. So, taking sound advice, that's what I drank, and we had a never-to-be-forgotten New Year celebration. We danced the night away, blissfully ignorant of what 1977 would bring. But, as friends kissed my cheek, the searing pain still screamed through my head.

The week after the Ball, my face began to swell and I couldn't bear to touch it. Since the antibiotics obviously weren't working, I agreed to have some X-rays, which showed that my sinuses were blocked, although I hadn't suffered a cold all winter; apart from my face, I was in very good health. Dr Perry, my doctor, suggested that I went to see a consultant at King Edward VII Hospital in Windsor, and an appointment was duly made with a Mr Wallace.

But before that was my birthday. Claire insisted on baking my cake and the boys helped her to decorate it. Chris and I sat in the lounge and the lights were switched off. We could hear giggles and excited laughter from the kitchen. Then the door was flung open and the room immediately transformed into brilliant light: my cake was covered with thirty-six lighted candles!

The three of them carried the cake to me singing 'Happy Birthday'. As their little faces were silhouetted against the wall and highlighted by the glow from the candles, I saw the joy in their eyes—mingled with mischief at having succeeded in getting thirty-six candles alight all at once. It reminded me of the Blackpool illuminations!

Three weeks later I went to see Mr Wallace. The X-rays showed up similar symptoms to before, so Mr Wallace suggested I had a sinus wash-out. When he was anaesthetising my nose he pressed on my face, and as my reaction (a muffled scream!) wasn't at all what he had expected he told me I would have to have an exploratory examination as soon as possible.

I think that was one of the busiest weeks of my life. I prepared evening meals and froze them, made a week's supply of rolls for Chris and Claire and arranged the week off from play school.

I explained carefully to the children what was happening and asked my mother to come to stay. I bought a present each for the children to open every morning for a week. The night before I left I was busy wrapping up twenty-one goodies and hiding them all over the house.

The next day I was admitted to Wexham Park Hospital and quickly made myself comfortable in my corner of the ward. My instant companion was a girl called Margaret who had a very painful ear. We were both rather bored, so we decided we would wander off down to the entrance hall and treat ourselves to a bar of chocolate and a cup of tea. No sooner had we warmed our seats than a young, pink nurse said, 'You two shouldn't be here, you are not allowed off the ward and Sister wants you!' I felt six years old as we trooped back to the ward and sat meekly on our beds. Sister was very sweet and suggested we didn't go on any more mystery tours, as she liked to keep her patients where she could see them.

Inevitably the time came for my turn to starve, bathe and don the sexy theatre gown. Margaret and I were both going down, so we sat up in bed with our paper knickers on our heads awaiting our injections.

Chapter Two

The nurses told me that Chris just sat there holding my hand. I was fast asleep and totally unaware of what was going on. I remember waking up and it was dark. There was something wet running down my neck! When I touched it my gown was soaking. The nurse came after my call and re-dressed my face. This seemed to go on throughout the night. I surely must be bleeding to death—but I was too tired to care. By the following morning my head felt numb, I couldn't feel anything and I was hungry. The nurse came and suggested that we get up for breakfast. Get up!

Everybody up! Margaret and I glided up the corridor to the dining room. It was full of men and women smiling, eating. 'Porridge, Mrs Piff?' That was more than I could take, so quick turn—I just made it back to bed. I told the nurse I felt faint and it must have been the blood I lost during the night! Foolish girl: the nurse explained that I was simply having ice packs on my cheek to keep the swelling down!

The operation had involved cutting under the gum on my top lip to enable Mr Wallace to investigate what was happening in my cheek and the surrounding area.

Early the following morning, Sister Smith came to my bed and said that Mr Wallace would like to speak to me. I walked along the corridor not feeling very confident at all, I suspected all was not well and ahead through the door lay the moment of truth.

Mr Wallace stood up when I walked into the room. He looked very tall in his white coat, as he smiled at me and asked me to sit in the chair opposite him. His voice was as gentle as his eyes and I immediately sensed that something was wrong.

The word cancer was left unsaid, but nevertheless I had a tumour in my sinus and I had the choice of either immediate surgery or radiation treatment. I say I had the choice, but what I mean is that it had to be decided between Mr Wallace and a Dr Paul Strickland as to what they felt best. Fortunately for me, Dr Strickland was holding a clinic the next day. I thanked Mr Wallace for telling me, stood up and left the room. The walk back to the ward was one of the strangest experiences I have ever had. I was completely calm, yet absolutely un-seeing. I was aware of the nurses and patients looking at me, yet I was encapsulated in my own thoughts, totally oblivious of what was going on around me. I reached my bed, which was surrounded by flowers and cards, and looked up at Ollie Octopus, a toy Claire had made for me. Reality suddenly came back and kicked me hard in the stomach. 'Oh my God!' I flung myself on to the bed and wept. Then, equally quickly, 'Christine' took over again, confident and determined. I dried my eyes and took stock of myself. 'So, I have cancer. Right. Well, I'll treat it like 'flu. We'll treat it and get over it.'

At visiting time I recognised Chris's footsteps as he came along the corridor. I didn't say a word, he took me in his arms, all we needed was each other.

Mr Wallace had, unknown to me, told Chris about my condition. In fact, at this time he knew more about it than I did. I made it very clear that I wanted all our friends to know I had this ghastly disease and to talk about it not in whispers, but confidently and openly. I believed that this was the only way to tackle cancer: to talk about it and give encouragement to other people whose attitude towards it was one of absolute horror and abject fear.

Strych, Strychnine, I couldn't remember who it was I was going to see. Sister Brookes came hurrying into the ward.

'Hurry up, Mrs Piff, we mustn't be late.' The clinic was crowded as usual, and I asked Sister Brookes if Dr Strychnine was nice. She turned pale (as pale as a West Indian can turn) and said, 'Don't, for goodness sake, call him that! His name is Dr Strickland!'

'Moses' (that's what he looked like, with his long white coat—longer than usual as he was rather short—and snow white hair that winged out at either side) was looking up at my X-rays and rubbing his chin as I walked in. The silence was unbearable. When I couldn't stand it any longer, I said, 'Looking at the funny pictures?'

On reflection it was a stupid thing to say, and Dr Strickland must have thought so too. He retorted, 'Not so funny, my dear. In fact, very serious ones.'

After that, I can't remember his exact words, but I was aware that again the word cancer was tactfully not mentioned, and vaguely wondered why. Briefly, however, I was to undergo six weeks daily radiation treatment at Mount Vernon Hospital. I detected a slight hesitation in his voice, then I heard:

'It will mean the loss of sight in your left eye.'

I was stunned and caught my breath. He carried on, 'We must start the treatment as soon as you are able.'

I heard my own voice clearly this time, 'How about tomorrow?'

Tomorrow came very rapidly. It was a long walk to the hospital lounge where I had to report for the ambulance. I was quite breathless when I arrived and I felt a bit wobbly in my high-heeled shoes, but they were such a pleasing change from slippers. There was a young boy of about seventeen or so on a stretcher with a nurse in attendance. I asked if I could sit in front with the driver. He was hesitant at first and said that it was a bit unusual but he thought it would be okay. It was a lovely journey, the sun was shining and I felt as if I was on a Sunday School outing.

At about eleven o'clock we arrived, and were deposited in the waiting room with lots of other people. It was a very old hospital, but the unit was brightly painted with pictures on the wall and flowers on the tables.

We waited and waited for what seemed like hours. Eventually I saw Dr Martin, Dr Strickland's registrar. He spent a long time drawing a detailed diagram of my head: measuring, drawing up a map, and marking in the area of my face where the radiation was to penetrate. I was fascinated by the detail and the care he took. I asked him what would happen to my skin. He said it would go a darker pink and wouldn't look very different.

'What about my eye? Is it because of the tumour I will lose my sight or is it the radiation?'

'The radiation, but if you keep your eye open for as long as you can without blinking, that will help.'

Dr Martin then took me to a little room where I lay on a very hard bed while a large piece of equipment was lowered over my head. Carefully the radiotherapist placed a glass shield over my face and used pieces of lead to protect other parts of my face. A pink pad was put directly on to my cheekbone and I was told to keep very still. She left the room and I could hear strange ticking sounds as the machine started up. A radio was on outside. I lay there listening to the music, thinking, what am I doing here? It was all over in a few minutes and I felt nothing at all. On Dr Martin's advice I kept my eye wide open and blinked as little as possible.

Outside I met up with the young boy again. He was looking awful. I asked him how he had got on but he could barely speak to me. It seemed he had no idea what was wrong with him. He'd had an operation on his thigh at Wexham Park Hospital and had then been sent along to Mount Vernon. He had just been told he had cancer and was terribly shocked.

I told him about myself and said that we should be grateful that they were doing something for us so quickly. This didn't cheer him up at all. Then I noticed he had a Chelsea Football Club badge on. I said, 'You don't support that rubbishy team do you?' There came a glimmer of reaction in his eyes at last and he began to chat to me.

We were at Mount Vernon until after 4pm, and were both feeling pretty well exhausted. It was less than a week since I had had surgery. The Sister came towards us both—by now the only two patients in the waiting room. She apologised for the wait for the ambulance and suggested we went and lay down in the treatment rooms. Everywhere was very still and quiet and as I lay there I slowly began to feel afraid and abandoned. I heard the clicking of receivers and the rasping voice of the receptionist.

I knew which one, a small inconsiderate woman with a sharp manner who seemed completely alien to her surroundings. Slowly I became more and more irritated. The telephone—of course! I jumped off the couch, struggled into my shoes, grabbed my bag and aimed for the receptionist's desk. 'Would you phone and get me a taxi, please. I can't hang around here all day.'

Flustered and bewildered by this strange demand from the fragile woman who had sat around all day, the poor dear turned puce and her eyes goggled.

'Err, you're from Wexham aren't you? The ambulance will be here very soon.'

'I don't want an ambulance. I want a taxi and I'm going home.'

Panic stations. Out came Dr Martin—and I promptly burst into tears. By the time I was calmed down and reassured, thank heaven, the ambulance had arrived.

How I walked along the corridor to Ward Eight I don't know. As I turned the corner, there was Nurse Hall, arms outstretched and the inmates all smiling and asking, 'Where the hell have you been? We were so worried about you.'

Simon had saved me a chip. Simon was six and was one of four little friends who were having their tonsils out. I had read them a story the night before and they had drawn me some lovely pictures. It helped fill the empty space of my own children. Simon had wrapped my chip up in a lovely drawing of a dinosaur. Now Wexham Park Hospital food is not bad at all, but a chip at least four hours old left a lot to be desired! Still, the satisfaction on Simon's face was well worth eating the chip for, and I *was* starving. After all, I hadn't eaten or drunk anything since breakfast.

Chris arrived that evening and he assured me the children were fine and looking forward to my home-coming.

He brought me a huge get-well card that the children from play school had made. They had all drawn around their hands and written their names inside the appropriate hand. It cheered me up no end after such a hard day. Chris taped this up on the window by my bed: it really was cheerful, and I felt very close to them all. As I looked up at the tiny hands I was filled with encouragement to survive the next six weeks.

It reminded me that I had a very important letter to write, for I realised that I wouldn't be going back to play school again for a very long time. This was a huge disappointment to me and I could hardly bear it. But my main aim was to survive the next six weeks and get them over as soon as possible. Roll on Easter!

Chapter Three

It seemed I had been in Wexham Park Hospital for weeks. I desperately wanted to return home. It was March and the bulbs were beginning to show their heads on the dull brown earth. Spring was on its way and I was impatient to see it.

Nothing is quite so boring as those last few hours after visitors have said their goodbyes. I had hoped to be going home, so was feeling exceptionally bored. Margaret wasn't feeling too well and was listening to the local radio station but it only made me cry. The previous night I had requested a popular song, 'When I need you.' We were all sitting up in our beds, headphones on, excitedly awaiting our requests and what happened—we all cried! But tonight I wandered restlessly up the corridor to the television room-cum-dining room, which was full of patients with cotton wool swabs under their noses, all watching a western.

'How about a drink?' Behind me stood a huge man with a very swollen face.

'Snap,' I said, pointing to my own swollen chops. 'I don't really fancy making chocolate and coffee now.'

'No, a real drink, come on.' So I walked past the children's ward, with the fair little 'angels' who should have been in bed, but definitely were not, and into another ward where the men were. They were drinking out of cans and eating crisps and chocolates. I thought I had been spoilt, but believe me, these men were having a super time.

John, who had invited me, asked what I would like to drink. 'Well, I'm a Guinness girl really, I don't really drink beer,' I replied.

Within fifteen minutes I was sitting in one of the armchairs, a can of Guinness in my hand, a pair of plastic glasses with a huge bandaged nose attached to it on my face and telling the bluest joke I knew. It was the most entertaining evening I had shared for a long time. The close friendships one made in an environment such as that was a small gift that you accepted gratefully. Each person knowing that we were all fighting our individual battles.

The night sister was great fun and didn't object to our party at all. I said my goodnights long after lights out and tip-toed my way past the sleeping children and the smelly television room. The lights were out in our small ward and I could see Margaret's curtains were drawn around her bed. I crept very quietly, didn't open my locker in case it made a noise and left my dressing gown on the bed. I lifted back the covers and there was a huge carrot and two oranges lying on my bed. I read the attached note, which said, 'Sweet dreams you dirty stop-out!'

The following day, when I arrived back at Ward Eight after my visit to Mount Vernon, I was greeted by Margaret, who was busily fiddling with a huge bunch of flowers. 'If you have any more bloody flowers—out of the window they go. We've no more vases, so I'm wrapping these up.' I looked and she had made an enormous bouquet out of the flowers from my window.

I asked her what on earth she was doing with them, confused and mystified by her behaviour. 'You're taking them home with you, Chris. We're both going home today. They can't stand us any longer.'

I was so excited I rushed to phone Chris at the office, and then sat down to wait. Waiting at Mount Vernon had seemed endless, but waiting for Chris was like waiting a whole lifetime. Eventually I couldn't stay awake. My bed had been stripped and remade so I couldn't lie on it. Kindly one of the other patients suggested I lay on top of her bed. So I was awakened by Chris shaking me gently saying, 'Come on, sleepyhead, I've come to take you home.'

As I walked through the front door I was greeted with great hugs from my mother. Nobody at all would believe I was my mother's daughter—I am tall and slim and Mummy is just five feet tall and very cuddly, with a mop of snow white hair and the constitution of an ox. I could see the anxiety on her face and realised how awful this must be for her. A cup of tea, to sit in my own chair and gaze at my treasures of home. It was a magical moment, like returning from a long holiday and realising the old homestead wasn't such a dump after all!

I felt the moment was right for me to discuss with the children about my cancer and what was going to happen in the next six weeks. I told them as simply as I could that I had a lump called cancer growing in my face. I couldn't just leave it there as it would grow bigger. The consultant at Wexham Park Hospital and the special cancer doctor from Mount Vernon Hospital were going to make the lump disappear by treating it with a very special machine which sent out rays of radiation. This was going to be done for the next six weeks. I didn't really understand it clearly myself yet, but felt it very necessary for the children's sake that they knew what was happening to their mummy.

Saturday morning. There's something special about Saturday, I don't know what it is, but I still have that super feeling that I had as a child—Saturday pictures and pocket money, sweets and getting dirty! Every Saturday I awaken with the same feeling, but this particular one I felt was very special. No radiation treatment for a start, so I could lie in.

The telephone rang. The word was round that I was out of hospital and home. The phone interrupted our day together but it was so lovely to be encouraged by so many well-wishers. In no time at all we had a rota system fixed for to-ing and fro-ing from Mount Vernon hospital for the next six weeks.

The children were very helpful and considerate. It was so lovely to hold them in my arms again and catch up on all their love. Chris had told them that if I was tired and needed to rest, it wasn't a good idea to have too many friends in the house playing. I felt guilty at this, as our home was always full of other people's children and I enjoyed it as much as they did. Chris didn't. I don't blame him, there's nowhere else to go if the house is littered with children. His refuge is to put on his headphones and hide behind the *Daily Telegraph!*

It was a wonderful day. I was so happy to be home and reunited with the children once more. They had taken it all in their stride and had coped admirably. Claire made me tea, and the boys really made an effort to be a little less noisy.

A friend had made us beef stroganoff for supper that night, and another friend, who is a pilot, had brought me some strawberries from somewhere in the Middle East. I felt thoroughly spoilt, but when I sat at the table and looked at my plate, absolute nausea came over me. I dismissed it as hunger and managed to eat some beef and even insisted on one strawberry. But the thought of food made my stomach contract. If I hadn't known better, I would have thought I was pregnant.

On Monday morning the radiographer told me that Dr Strickland and Mr England wanted to see me. I was ushered into the room and sat upon a chair. Dr Strickland examined my face and left nostril and invited Mr England to do the same. Then my X-rays were shown on a screen and I peeped through the gap to see what was going on, but the nurse obviously disapproved of this and closed up the curtain. As if I could understand a word they were talking about! After all, it was *my* face they were discussing and I wanted to know what was going on. Afterwards I told 'Moses' about the beef and strawberries and asked if his radiation treatment was to blame. He looked at his colleagues and nodded his head. 'Yes, you can blame us for that.' I thanked him very much and asked what I should do. 'I suggest the next time you have strawberries you give them to me.' For the first time a giggle bubbled up from inside me—he was human after all.

My next step was to visit yet another specialist. A charming middle-aged lady came out and immediately put me at my ease. My first impression was that I was entering another world, a world of space odyssey. There was an enormous dial on the wall surrounded by numbers. In the centre of the room was a couch which could be raised or lowered and moved from left to right, all at the press of a button. Above this was a large piece of apparatus which held what turned out to be a camera. Basically what it did was to take an X-ray, film it and print it out on to a television screen. The viewer could then see the tumour and treat it with what they decided was adequate radiation.

I climbed on to the couch, which was as hard as nails. Now, if I lie flat on my back I always cross my ankles, and as I had my knee-high boots on and had to lie for what seemed like hours absolutely flat with toes pointing to the ceiling, it almost finished off my poor back. When I couldn't take the strain any longer, I let my poor old ankles relax and both feet fell outwards. I thought to myself, I must look dead. In fact, not only do I look dead, I feel dead!

The confident lady returned. She told me to stay completely still, and not to move a muscle. On my nose she placed a long piece of wire—I think it was wire because it was very stiff, yet pliable. This was bent down the centre of my forehead, down my nose and then stuck out at the end. I could see my silhouette against the wall—it looked horrific. I would win first prize on Hallowe'en night. The wickedest witch of them all.

After the careful positioning of the camera the lights were switched off and I was in total darkness. I mean not just dark, but absolute blackness. I didn't feel frightened, I just wished I could see the picture that she could see. After a while she returned and said it was fine. My nasal contraption was removed and so was something that had been placed under my neck to support my head. This pulled my hair and I flicked it back over my shoulder. This must have drawn her attention to my hair.

'You have such thick, long hair, you'll be able to cover the patch where the radiation goes through with your own hair.' I must have given her a very gormless look and she said, 'Haven't they told you about your hair? The radiation kills the cells of your hair and you will lose it, I'm afraid.'

It wasn't the best way to spend a Monday morning anyway, and to be told my hair was going to fall out did little to cheer me up.

I began to get up, but she said, 'Don't go yet, Mrs Piff, Jeff is coming in to make a mask of you.' My mind boggled! Jeff was very young, but he was very clever. He proceeded to make a perfect wire mask of my head. It seemed a strange thing to do, but mine was not to reason why.

23

Enter the lady again, armed with a red pen. I had to lie very still as my face was measured with another weird instrument, and then little kisses were put on the outer edges of the area to be radiated. I did look pretty! Rather like a hectic morning doing finger painting at play school. At least it was something to laugh about. From now on, no more washing or cleaning my face, which obviously meant no more make-up. In fact I had been told by the therapist not to wash at all for the next six weeks—everyone up wind of Christine!

On Tuesday's journey I was feeling really happy. I had received nearly a week's radiation, and with only five more to go, it wasn't that bad at all.

'Mrs Piff, nurse would like to see you this morning. Today you are to have an injection and then your treatment twenty minutes afterwards.'

I felt sick. Injection, where? In my face? I'm not that brave. Sue was my chauffeur that particular morning and she looked positively pale round the gills. I was shown into a little room and the nurse asked me to pull my pants down as the injection was better given standing up in the upper buttock.

I thought to myself, right, I'm standing up in front of the children at play group and I'm showing them how easy it is to have an injection. As I felt the initial jab of the needle enter, I carried on a conversation with the children. I could feel whatever it was go searing down my leg and I imagined it belting around my bloodstream. It was over in a few seconds.

I had my treatment as usual, and asked the radiotherapist what drug I had been given and why. She kindly explained the drug and said that it helped to destroy the cancer cells. I was to have twelve of these injections during the treatment on Tuesdays and Fridays.

When I got home, Mummy made me a cup of tea so that I would be rested before the tribe arrived home. I came downstairs and sat in the lounge. The sensation that I had was so hard to describe. My mind was present, but my body felt numb. I could hardly move my limbs at all. I moved to sit on a chair and look out of the window. My arms hurt so much I didn't know where to put them to be comfortable. I felt like two people, my mind was calm and undisturbed yet my physical body seemed in absolute turmoil. The sensation was horrible and I became more and more frightened as it remained with me.

Chris was home early and I tried to explain to him how I felt. It was obviously the drug that had created this sensation. I tried to fight it for as long as I could, my arms felt like enormous tree trunks and try as I could I was unable to lift them.

Chris took me in his arms and carried me upstairs to bed. I cried bitterly. I was so frightened, there was no way I could use my psychoprophylaxis (mind over matter) to help me to distract myself from this agony. I felt ashamed that I could not cope with it. I didn't want Chris to know how really terrified I was. I knew my strength was his strength and without it we wouldn't be able to cope with the following weeks.

The next morning I awoke and the nightmares of the previous day were but a memory, no trace was left. I was up and singing, the sheer relief that I felt better an overwhelming joy. I became aware of every sensation, the children, their love and their laughter, Mummy's kindness to us all and her infinite understanding. But most of all I thanked God for Chris's tolerance and compassion, and our deep, deep love for each other.

I was two weeks into my treatment now. The radiation made me feel very tired and I slept for two hours every afternoon. As I was up at seven and left for hospital at eight, my day was pretty occupied. I spent hours just looking out of the window and willing the plants to grow. I had never had so much time to spend before just sitting and dreaming. The blue tits were paying regular visits to the nesting box. I am an enthusiastic gardener and enjoyed raking up the leaves and preparing for the next season's flowers. But this year that would have to wait.

It was Saturday morning and I had recovered from my previous day's injection and I was brushing my hair. I pretended to ignore that the brush was full of hair. Suddenly I became aware of a tiny bump, like an ulcer, on the tip of my tongue. Dr Perry had called to see me during the week and asked if my mouth was sore. Strange, I thought, I wonder if there is any connection. By mid-day my tongue was covered in tiny eruptions, so I phoned the surgery. As Dr Perry was out I explained this strange symptom to another doctor. He suggested I didn't drink anything hot or cold and said there was nothing else I could do about them. He suspected they were to do with the radiation treatment.

From that moment on the ulcers, as I called them, grew more and more painful. I couldn't wait to go back to the hospital to find an explanation—and a prescription to make my mouth more comfortable.

It was Wednesday before I saw 'Moses', who explained that these were not ulcers but radiation burns. He prescribed a white, revolting-looking substance to wash my mouth out with. I was so starving hungry, I think I would have done anything to enable me to eat something, so I stood over the kitchen sink, and poured the mixture on to a spoon. I took a deep breath and put the liquid into my mouth. My entire mouth felt as if it was on fire! With one spit the white liquid was rejected down the kitchen sink, and furiously I washed it away. I was still faint with hunger, so I cracked two eggs in a bowl, added a teaspoon of sugar, half a pint of milk and whisked them up. I poured the mixture into one of Chris's beer mugs and sat down. Mummy, who had been witnessing all this, never said a word. I looked at her and then at the glass. I lifted it up and took the longest drink I could. Perhaps it wasn't too bad. After all, at least it was food.

Someone then suggested I try Complan and this I did, but I could still feel the texture of the granules on my tongue. It was like an abrasive. So was everything else I tried—cheese soufflé, steamed fish, baked egg custard, baby food. Chris tried to liquidise some beef and gravy, but this was agony to put in my mouth. For days I was living on milk and raw eggs and junket. I promised everyone that one day I would invite them all to dinner and I would have an enormous steak and they would have raw eggs and junket!

As the weeks went by I was getting weaker and weaker. Dorothy, a very good friend and dietician, gave me some iron and vitamin tablets to take, and made out a high protein menu that I should eat. But it was impossible to eat anything. Eventually, my mouth became so sore that I couldn't even drink the eggs. All I could take was small sips of warm milk. Having started this adventure at seven stone six pounds I was not too happy at losing weight. I looked like a bag of bones, my shoes were too big and rubbed blisters on my toes. My hair was noticeably thinner. The left side of my face was bright red and my lips were so dry and cracked it even hurt to smile.

Meanwhile Spring was on its way! Every day I watched the hedges unfurl their little green leaves and the birds beginning to sing. I was so aware of nature and life being born again. It seemed so cruel to me to think that I might be dying. It hadn't crossed my mind before, but now I was beginning to feel so ill. I sat one evening in the lounge with Mummy while Chris was at a meeting. Mummy phoned Daddy and I heard her saying, 'Oh, she's fine, a bit better today. No, not eating, she looks like a puff of wind would blow her away.'

I started to cry. I shook and shook from deep down inside. Mummy came to me and knelt in front of me. She cupped my face in her hands. 'What's the matter Christine?'

'Oh Mummy, I don't want to die.'

I decided that night that I really should discuss the possibility of my dying with Chris.

It was the saddest moment I have ever endured. Words wouldn't come, and we both lay in each other's arms and cried ourselves to sleep.

At that time I was waking every twenty minutes throughout the night as my mouth and throat dried up, and couldn't make saliva so I had to drink a sip of water. My right hip was red and sore where I continually heaved myself up to drink, but at least this took my mind off my face. I tried to lie on my back, but couldn't sleep. I could hear Chris's deep breathing beside me and I put my arm over him. What would he do if I were to die? How could he cope? What would happen to the children? Chris's mother had died when he was four, when she was thirty-four, and she had four children and had just given birth to twins.

Chris's life had been continuous turmoil, numerous schools, different homes and eventually a step-mother he loathed. We met when we were at school, although he left before I did and we hardly ever met again until I was eighteen. I used to meet a crowd of friends on a Saturday morning for coffee. Inevitably I bumped into Chris and his friends. We would stand chatting to one another for hours trying to outdo one another making puns—our sense of humour was the initial attraction. From then on we saw each other regularly and eventually married in June 1962, when we were both twenty-one.

As I lay there remembering all the wonderful times we'd shared, my whole life seemed gloriously happy. We had never experienced any tragedy, the saddest thing was when Chris's father died. We had chosen to have three children. I in fact had wanted four, but Chris had said, enough is enough, and I accepted it. Life to me was so precious, I enjoyed everything I did so much. Why should I die? Just because I have cancer. Why, when I have so much to live for? I have so much more to do. I'm not going to. I *won't*. I will fight with every ounce of strength I have.

I lay there feeling so angry with the world and then an inner calm came over me and I felt at ease. There was the strongest sensation of peacefulness and I heard in my head my own voice saying, you're not going to die. You have too much to do.

Chapter Four

I had now been receiving radiation treatment for a month. I was seeing Dr Strickland regularly and had complained about not being able to eat because my mouth was so sore. He didn't seem concerned, in fact he approved of the condition, and said how successfully the treatment was going and he prescribed two days' rest. This meant no treatment for four days! I was so excited, rather like a child being sent home from boarding school.

As ill as I felt, I was determined that we should do something special during the weekend. I awoke early on Saturday and prodded Chris.

'How about going to the sea-side?' He sat up in surprise. 'Are you sure you feel up to it? It would be lovely.'

It was early April, a surprisingly beautiful time of the year. The journey to the coast took only an hour. The children were so excited as it was our first family outing of the year. We always preferred seaside trips either early or late in the year, as once the summer arrives it is too crowded to enjoy it in comfort.

The sea looked rough and cross and smacked the rocks with indignation as if it, too, were impatient for the warmer weather to arrive. The wind was blowing and I was bullied into wearing so many clothes and scarves that I felt top-heavy. We walked a short way along the front to the promenade and I began to wilt. I found a convenient rock and sat back, watching the four of them throwing stones into the sea.

There is something about being near the sea that makes everything else fall into insignificance. We had spent so many happy day trips here. Even before little Dominic arrived it held so many sweet memories for us all. I felt satisfied at having made the effort to come. We walked back to the car and I sipped my milk.

'We'll come back again in the summer, Mummy, and you can throw stones in.'

'Yes, Dominic, we will, I promise.'

It was Easter, which I enjoy nearly as much as Christmas, and this year it was an even more important event than usual as I had only one week more to go at Mount Vernon.

The house was full of plants and flowers—it looked more like a florist's shop than a home. I had received get-well cards every day in the post and the lounge wall was covered from floor to ceiling. I still couldn't get over the feeling of amazement that so many people cared. It made the children realise what friendship really meant. A handful of cards arrived from play school by post, addressed Auntie Chris, c/o Uncle Chris, followed by my address. The postman must have wondered what had hit us. The cards were all hand done with drawings of me and covered in kisses. I couldn't wait to get back to them and pick up where I had left off, I missed them all so much.

Mary, a friend I had made when Matthew was at play school, came to see me and she brought me the most beautiful Easter egg I had ever seen! She knew that I couldn't eat it, but said that if I knew it was there it would make me even more determined to get better and eat it.

Suddenly, it was my last day at Mount Vernon. I couldn't believe it, I kept on thinking, they are going to tell me to come back next week. I had been given four days' 'rest' from treatment and had Good Friday off and Easter Monday, so I had six days that I called 'extra' to go.

I said a fond farewell to the butterflies on the ceiling of the treatment room and I skipped out! It was over, seven whole weeks. I was better. I didn't feel it, but the psychological significance of the final treatment made me feel as if I was on cloud nine.

Before I left I saw Mark, the boy with the bad leg. I had thought he had finished his treatment, so was surprised to see him. Apparently, he was to have extra drugs and treatment as his cancer was spreading. This worried me, as I had every faith in the radiation treatment being able to contain and destroy the disease. I wished Mark every good fortune and hoped he would soon be well.

I also saw the radiotherapist, who told me, 'The radiation continues to work even though you are not having any more treatment. This means that your mouth won't begin to recover for another two weeks.'

Pop, went my balloon. But oh well, what's another two weeks? I was given a prescription for some cream to put on my face, which by now was purple and black in places. My hair was very thin, and I had lost all the hair an inch above my ear to the centre back of my head and down to my neck. It was jolly chilly. I weighed five stone by now and didn't need a bra, but I had lovely long fingernails—it must have been all that milk. All I had to do now was get fit again. I'd show them. When I next saw Dr Strickland I was determined he wouldn't recognise me.

Doctor Perry was very good and came to see me every week. He looked at my left eye to see if there was any deterioration, but could see none. Or if he could, he didn't tell me. I was determined to keep that eye as long as I could. I hadn't blinked during the treatment and had prayed and prayed to God to help me keep the sight in my eye. I wore glasses anyway, and the thought of losing the sight in it I found abhorrent.

The week went by and I tried dunking a biscuit in my tea and it worked. It was uncomfortable but I could eat it. Next, I made some milky porridge which I covered in syrup and sugar. Gradually, I progressed from porridge to omelette and soufflé, and, with the guidance of Dorothy, I ate high protein foods. I drank hot chocolate and Complan and my luxury was to suck a chocolate button. The excitement that ran through the entire household was so infectious. I was having phone calls from friends saying, 'We heard you ate an egg, how wonderful!' Sadly though, I found that I had lost my sense of taste. I couldn't tell if things were sweet or not, everything was completely bland.

Chris's Uncle Reg had decided he would build a chicken house and keep chickens. We had daily phone calls to see if his chickens had laid any eggs, as he had promised that I should have the first one. Well, it turned out that poor Uncle Reggie's dreams were not to come true. He was awakened very early one morning by the crowing of a very noisy cockerel. He went out to check his six hens and they all greeted him with a dawn chorus of cock-a-doodle-doos!

It was nearly the end of April when I had made an amazing recovery. My mouth wasn't completely better but I could eat. I drank three pints of milk a day and continued with the raw eggs. Whenever Dr Perry came to see me I began to think he really shouldn't be wasting his precious time visiting me. I felt I was well on the road to recovery, and if I needed him I would phone. However, I did wonder why I hadn't heard from Mount Vernon. Surely they would want to see me again. Doctor Perry said not to worry, give them a month and then contact them. So when an appointment to see Dr Strickland arrived I breathed a sigh of relief. The thought of seeing him again filled me with such determination and anticipation I could hardly wait.

But before then, friends had volunteered to look after the children so that Chris and I could go away. The weather was much milder and I had already spent odd afternoons in the garden. The thought of a holiday abroad and all that sunshine was very appealing, but I knew I wouldn't enjoy it if the children were not with us. We decided we would try to go away for a week-end—after all Chris needed a reward for all his hard work and untiring effort in running the house and children, and keeping me happy.

I was feeling so happy and much healthier. I still had a sleep in the afternoons and found this to be a great healer. As Matthew's tenth birthday was coming up I suggested we had a treat, as I couldn't cope with a party of ten-year-olds. One has to be really fit for that. Matthew gave his birthday a great deal of thought and then announced that he would like to go to Avebury Downs, where the Roman ruins are and walk to the Long Barrow. Oh well, we did suggest a treat, so there was no backing out of it. Claire had been to Avebury with her school and had enthused so much about it. Chris and I share a common interest in archaeology and some of this had obviously rubbed off on the children. At least the treat would be interesting to all of us and perhaps improve our minds—if that's possible. It certainly gave me something to look forward to, and took my mind off the appointment with Dr Strickland.

Chapter Five

When the day arrived to go back to the hospital I woke up and wondered why I felt so excited. The children came in to see me before they went to school as they usually did, and we had cuddles all round. Chris packed them off and instructed them to go to a neighbour after school, in case we were held up at the hospital.

It was a lovely day, the sun was shining and the trees were so beautifully green and fresh. I carefully chose what to wear and took care in my make-up and hair. At last I was ready, and Chris and I walked out to the car. I felt so well and proud. We had survived the past five months of turmoil and overcome the awful threat which had hung over us.

The waiting room was crowded, the only two available seats at the corner of the annexe. We recognised familiar faces walking up and down the corridor. Most of the patients were older people, looking sad and introverted. The nurses and the receptionists all seemed to have a purpose and bustled around discharging their duties with smiling faces, carrying folders and looking efficient.

Eventually, my name was called and I walked in. The room was very large. To the right as I entered was a long table covered in apparatus. Standing beside the table were Dr Strickland and Dr Martin, his registrar. To my surprise Mr Wallace, my consultant, was there too.

'Sit down Mrs Piff. How are you?' Dr Strickland asked as he came and sat in front of me and stared at my face as if he could see through me. He examined my eye and my nostrils, stood up and removed the chair without saying a word and went across to Mr Wallace.

'Well, what's wrong, aren't you pleased with me?' I could feel these words in my head. Why don't they say something? Dr Strickland looked at Mr Wallace and then back at me.

'Well, that's stage one over. Now we move to stage two.' He extended his arm with open palm to Mr Wallace.

I looked at Mr Wallace in amazement, as he said, 'I would like you to come into hospital on Monday and we will do some tests. Then on Friday I will operate on your face.'

I felt as if I was made of glass and he had raised a hammer and smashed me into a million pieces. He continued to speak, but I couldn't hear. I was destroyed. I wanted to cry out, No, no, this can't be true, it can't, not to me. Oh God, let this be a dream. Not after all I've endured.

Mr Wallace's mouth stopped moving. The nurse put her arm around me, took me out and sat me on a seat in the corridor. Just around the corner, six feet away was Chris. How could I tell him? I sat there in a daze, trying to comprehend the meaning of it all. I was in complete despair, unable to move or to think. I don't know how long I sat there.

It was no use. I had to share my burden with Chris. I stood up, took a deep breath and walked around the corner. He looked up, and on seeing my expression his face was motionless. He put his arm around me and we walked. I couldn't speak, the lump in my throat grew bigger and bigger until I couldn't bear it any more. We clung to each other in the middle of the reception area, hundreds of people walking about, queueing, waiting, but I didn't notice them. All I could see were the tears in Chris's eyes as I told him. He was like a mountain. Just to be with him I gradually became calm. We walked back to the seats and waited. We didn't speak, it was a silence of inner stillness and incomprehensible torture of our imagination at what lay before us.

After a while a nurse came up and explained that Mr Wallace wanted me to see Mr Issa, the oral surgeon, straight away. So we waited and in due course Mr Wallace asked us to join him. It was a small room with an old-fashioned dentist chair in the middle of it. Mr Wallace introduced me to Mr Issa and I sat in the chair. Mr Issa was pleasant and friendly as he examined my teeth and commented on how the dentist and I must be friends as I had so many fillings! I began to relax a little. The atmosphere here wasn't so 'electric'. 'They are fine,' he said at last.

'So they should be,' I replied. 'It may seem silly, but what am I doing at the dentist anyway?'

Mr Issa looked at Mr Wallace, who in turn looked at Chris. It was Mr Wallace's turn to speak. 'I'm afraid we have to remove your left upper jaw and palate.'

I swallowed. How much more could I take? 'But I hate false teeth,' was all I could say. I couldn't contain myself any longer. I buried my face in my hands and let the tears flow. The three men just looked at each other and remained silent. I composed myself at last and climbed out of the chair.

Mr Wallace said, 'Ward Eight. Monday. I will operate on Friday the 13th.'

Chris looked surprised and said, 'I hope you're not superstitious.'

'I'm not, if you're not,' replied Mr Wallace. 'And there's no likelihood of any black cats in the operating theatre!'

Slowly I began to try to organise myself into planning the following five days. Chris phoned Mummy and asked if she would move back to us again. It must have been quite a shock for her to realise that her only daughter was to undergo facial surgery. But, in her usual manner, she accepted it with calm patience and said that she would be there for as long as we wanted her. It was a blessed relief, knowing we had her to rely on. I knew the children would be secure and their lives would continue undisturbed whilst Grandma was there, and this took a great load off my mind.

That week, the house was never empty of friends. They were distraught at the future prospects for me and tried to encourage me as much as they could. On one morning a friend, who was not particularly close, called to see me. She had brought gifts for the children, which touched me deeply. She insisted on helping to get lunch for the children, and we were completely at ease with one another. As I said goodbye to her, I admired a necklace she was wearing.

Immediately she took it off and put it around my neck. 'I made it myself, and it would please me if you would have it. I didn't know what you would like, as you seem to have everything.' She hugged me, and left.

Sunday was Matthew's birthday and my last day with the family for a while. It was sunny but windy, an ideal day for our treat. Matthew was so excited, we had given him an alarm clock and he was well pleased with it. I hoped we wouldn't have it sounding out its fearful yell every hour throughout the day. No need to worry. It was wound up and placed on his bedside table ready for Monday morning.

As I walked out to the car with our picnic, Claire was waiting for me with a camera. I was wearing large sunglasses, as my left eye had started to water and I thought the dark glasses would help. I stood by the car and she said, 'Smile, Mummy'. I looked at her and wanted to fling my arms around her and hold her close to me. This photograph was the last one of me as I was. I look at it now and remember the lovely day we had. The long walk up to the Long Barrow. The lovely view of the fields full of corn, stretching as far as we could see. The promise of summer and brighter days. Matthew and Dominic rolly-pollied down the hillside, and were covered in grass, their squeals of laughter breaking the silence. Claire walked next to me knowing that tomorrow would be a different day altogether.

The children didn't mind me going into hospital again, they said that they had enjoyed themselves with Grandma and it wouldn't be long. I didn't know how long I would be away for this visit, but they could come and see me and write to me. Fortunately, they were tired after their busy day and I cuddled each one of them and said their prayers. Matthew said they should have a kiss for at least two of the weeks I would be away, so forty-two kisses later I tucked them up, and told them all to look under their pillows tomorrow bedtime.

Monday morning was just like any other Monday. Matthew's alarm had gone off and he didn't know how to stop it. Queues for the loo, the usual rush to leave the house by 8.30. I promised the children I would leave with them in the car. We dropped off

Claire first and then said goodbye to the boys. I confidently shouted, 'Bye, boys, see you soon.'

Chris drove away and I turned to see them running into school.

Chapter Six

The long walk to Ward Eight seemed endless. Nurse Hall was standing by the office. With a beaming smile she said, 'We've been waiting for you, Christine. We have a special room for you—we thought you would like the privacy. But you can have your old bed in the ward until Friday if you would prefer.'

How considerate they were. 'Oh no, to save the trouble of changing I'll have the little room,' I said. I followed Sister Smith into a small square room. It was very pleasant—one wall was all window, covered by a yellow curtain; on the opposite wall was a fitted wardrobe and washbasin. The bed sat in between the two, with a locker to the right of the bed by the window. It was stark and sterile, but I knew it wouldn't take long to make it look lived in.

I unpacked my nightclothes and dressing gowns. The children's photograph was put on display and Olly Octopus placed over my name above the bed. Chris had to go. He would be in to see me later, but I hated saying goodbye. I walked back along the corridor with him and we parted with just a smile.

Sister wanted to see me in the office. She gave me a bracelet to put on my wrist. It had my name and date of birth on it. It reminded me of when I was a little girl and my Grandpa took me to the cattle market. I can hear the pigs squealing as the man put a metal clip through their ears. Grandpa said that it really didn't hurt them and I shouldn't cry. It didn't hurt me when Sister put the bracelet on, it just made my heart miss a beat.

We made friendly conversation and then she came to the point and said, 'Now, I'm going to tell you what will happen to you. It's a wonderful operation. They cut the upper lip to the nose, then around the nose up to the corner of your eye and around to the outer edge. The skin is then pulled back and this enables them to remove the bone. The left side of your palate will be removed. This will be replaced by an obturator which Mr Issa will make for you. This afternoon Mr Issa would like to see you. Any questions? Do you understand?'

'No questions.' I just felt numb.

'Dr Goldstein is your anaesthetist and you couldn't be in better hands. If I was having an operation, he's the man I would choose.' Sister Smith was being so kind. There wasn't much response I could make. I had come to terms with having to lose part of my face in order to survive. How they did it wasn't up to me. I was in their hands completely. I put my absolute trust in Mr Wallace and his team. After all, if it weren't for them I wouldn't be there.

Mr Issa was bright and cheerful. I sat in the chair and a plastic bib was placed around my neck. My upper teeth were then fitted to a sort of circular metal mousetrap that could be adjusted to fit any size. The nurse then baited the trap with her magic mixture and it was placed in my mouth—it tasted pretty horrible. I had to wait for this to set, whilst Mr Issa made polite conversation. The same procedure followed for my lower jaw.

Then came the nasty bit. Mr Issa showed me some teeth. They were individual teeth, all the same size, but varying in colour.

'Now, we have to match these up with your own natural teeth colour.' Ugh! I found this quite macabre. There I was with a healthy set of teeth and having to choose the colour of my false ones. Perish the thought! 'Here's a mirror, now see if you can match them up. I know—even better, go to the technician's room. The light is better there.'

The nurse helped me out of the chair and took me across the room to the lab. Here I met Harry and John. I had my mirror in one hand and my 'teeth' in the other. I must have looked so stupid. If ever I wanted to run away from anything before, it was nothing compared to this trepidation I felt.

It had to be done. I told Harry it wouldn't take long, the

yellowest one would probably match mine. I compared them and on John's advice they agreed that I had chosen the correct colour. Then we went back to Mr Issa, and Harry showed him the shade. The number was recorded. Mr Issa asked if I would go along to the photographer and have some close-up shots of my teeth taken.

'Yes, I'll go now. Only promise me when I wake up on Friday after the operation I will have my teeth in place.' Mr Issa promised, and said that without the obturator I wouldn't be able to speak. I didn't take much notice of this at the time.

The photographer recognised me. I had had a photograph taken on leaving the hospital in February. He asked how I was and what was now happening. I told him the story of the radiation and how I was now having these photographs taken to help Mr Issa in making the obturator. 'How sad,' he said. 'I'm so sorry. Smile, please.'

Chris visited me every day and was obviously getting more anxious as Friday approached. I was so eager to know what was happening at home. Friends and neighbours were planning the Jubilee street party, that sounded fun. It was something for the children to look forward to. I had put a bag of one pound's worth of five pence coins under the children's pillows. Chris said that it was like finding buried treasure, they were so excited. He didn't know what had pleased them most, having a pound in five pence coins, or the little bag they were in! I think Chris was disappointed that he didn't have one under his pillow.

My little room was now beginning to look like home. The windowsill was covered in cards and flowers. The weather had suddenly decided it was nearly summer and the sun was very warm. We took chairs outside and sat and sunbathed in the garden. But there's no peace for the wicked. X-rays. Along the corridor I trotted into the X-ray room. The radiologist recognised my name and asked how I was. Everyone was so interested. I told her of the operation on Friday and I can remember her saying, 'My mother had a friend who had her palate removed, but don't worry, she learned to speak again.'

Again it didn't really register at the time, it just slotted into my subconscious.

The evening before the operation, I was determined to enjoy my supper, as I didn't know when I would next sit down and eat a meal. Chris arrived with cards and gifts and hundreds of kisses from the children. Our friends, Ken and Janette, had volunteered to take Claire, Matthew and Dominic away for the weekend. It was a wonderful idea, as it took the children out of the environment where anxiety would obviously be rife and left Chris free to visit me without having to think about them. We were both very relieved.

The conversation was light-hearted and we joked about the operation. I insisted that the following day I was going to get out of bed, even if I just walked around it and climbed in on the other side. I couldn't wait for the day to come, the sooner it was over the better. I really had to persuade Chris to leave me. I tried to make him feel confident, but I knew that as he looked at my face to smother it in kisses, he was looking at it for the last time.

I ran a glorious, deep bath. The bath in the hospital was super. But you couldn't lie back in it, or else you would go under! I soaked and sang every play school song I knew. It sounded wonderful, though it did occur to me that the other patients might not appreciate it. But they were all watching television anyway, so I hoped they hadn't heard! I put on my prettiest nightdress and a pale blue dressing gown. I brushed out my long hair and creamed my face. After all, it needed all the help it could get. I looked at my left eye in the steaming bathroom mirror. 'I'm sorry, eye, I tried my hardest to keep you, but if you've got to go, you've got to go.'

That evening Dr Goldstein came in and introduced himself. He examined me, and asked me if I was worried about tomorrow.

'It's no use me worrying is it? I am in your care, I leave it all to you,' I said.

He seemed surprised at my attitude, and reassured me that he would give me an anaesthetic which would not make me sick, as the previous one had. He gave me two tablets to take before I went to bed and he guaranteed I would sleep like a baby. I immediately liked Dr Goldstein, his whole manner was constructive and helpful and gave me confidence. I wished that Chris had met him.

The night nurse came into my room carrying a kidney shaped bowl. 'For you Mrs Piff. Penicillin injection.'

Confidently I exposed my left hip. 'The injections I had at Mount Vernon, I'll never forget, so this one should be easy,' I bragged to the nurse. It served me right. The injection went searing at top speed down my leg. I thought she had stabbed me! It was awful, I couldn't lie there, so I jumped up and down the room exclaiming, 'Bloody hell, nurse what was that?'

Friday the 13th was a beautiful day. A day full of life and promise. I lay there gazing out of the window, my thoughts automatically turning to Chris and the children. How much I loved them and needed them. I was aware also of how they loved and needed me. Could they cope if I should die? Dismiss those thoughts! Life was never so precious to me as I lay there, scrubbed and sterile, ready for the skilful team of surgeons. My senses were overflowing. I had to write to Chris and tell him how desperately I needed him, but most of all how much I loved him.

I propped the letter up on my locker where I could see it, next to the photograph of Claire, Matthew and Dominic.

Sister Smith came to give me my pre-med. 'See you later, Christine, good luck.' I lay there dreaming of sweet memories and a face with two hazel eyes.

A familiar voice whispered in my head. It was a long way off and was very faint. I recognised it as the voice of Sister Brookes.

'You've still got it, Christine. You've got your eye.'

My immediate reaction was not of excitement as one would expect, but of delight in hearing that familiar voice. But no sooner had I taken it in than it was gone again and I can't remember any more.

I was unaware of where I was, I could feel nothing and see nothing, total darkness. I couldn't remember anything that had happened previously, it was a state of physical insensibility.

Unknown to me, Chris spent hours beside me waiting for some sign of life, apart from the bleep, bleep monitoring my heart beat. I can't remember his voice or him touching me, I only know that I was aware that he was there. Once I lifted my index finger on my right hand and waved to him. It didn't occur to me why I couldn't see—it didn't seem to worry me unduly either—but I wanted to see Chris.

The effort I put into lifting my right eyelid was such a struggle, but briefly, for one fleeting second, before it closed shut again, I saw him. His eyes were shining and they smiled at me. He was all in white and he had a hat and a mask on. Then, total darkness again.

I became aware of voices, unfamiliar voices. I heard their footsteps, one of them wore wooden sandals that flopped and banged on the floor. The other one had soft shoes and a soft voice. They wet my mouth with something and washed me. In between the darkness came this pattern of care, and I realised I was not in Ward Eight. I still didn't remember the operation. I became aware of something over my face. I raised my hand slowly to touch what ever it was. It felt strange and unfamiliar, so I pulled it away and it moved over my chin. The nurse replaced it. I then became aware of my left arm. It felt heavy and I wanted to move it. I couldn't, but I was determined to. Something was stinging in my arm. Again, the nurse was there.

'Keep your arm straight, Christine, there's a drip in it.'

My right hand felt over my body. I was naked. I felt rubber pads with tubes coming from them. There was something in my neck, all taped up with what felt like elastoplast. I wriggled my toes. At least I could feel them. It felt lovely, I wanted to stretch, but I couldn't move my arm. My hand felt my left leg and my thigh was wrapped in what felt like crêpe bandage. I pulled at the object over my face. I didn't like it, I wished they wouldn't keep putting it on my face. No sooner did I pull it off, than it was put on again.

I remember being disturbed by voices, one was a man's voice. 'They are too long, cut them off.' A nurse protested and said she wouldn't. A hand lifted my hand and I realised they meant my fingernails! I took the male hand in mine and tapped the back of it. I heard a laugh and I pulled the 'thing' off my face again.

'The mask is worrying her, Doctor. She keeps pulling it off.'

'Take it away then, it's best not to distress her.' It was a man's voice again but not Mr Wallace. I felt happier at having the mask removed and more comfortable.

'Hello Christine, let's see how you are today.' I was turned over on to my side and the physiotherapist started beating the living daylights out of me. I wanted to laugh even though I was still in my dark world. The same sensation was there, I knew someone was present, but it wasn't Chris. They were standing to the left of me. I stirred and I recognised the soft voice of Mr Wallace. I held up my hand and he took it in his. It was then I remembered everything.

One of the nurses came to say goodnight. 'Be a good girl, see you tomorrow.'

I strained and strained my eyelid and slowly, slowly, it gradually opened.

'I can see you,' I cried! Her beaming smile shone over me and I was exhilarated. We both wept and another nurse came in.

'She can see us,' said the nurse happily. 'Goodbye, see you tomorrow.'

I lay there, letting my eye gradually become accustomed to the light. It suddenly dawned on me that the voice I had just heard didn't sound like my voice at all. In fact it sounded more like mumbled grunts than a voice. My eye closed and my tongue explored my mouth. It felt awful and dry. It was a strange sensation, my mouth felt so unnatural. I realised I had the obturator in and the upper teeth were Mr Issa's 'specials'. They were not level with my other teeth and felt very uncomfortable.

The following day I could open my eye more easily. I felt my head and I had a bandage all over my head and the left side of my face. A bright breezy nurse came on duty who washed me and insisted I have my own night clothes on. Two other nurses came to move the drip from my arm and put it in at my wrist. I had moved about too much and it made the skin very sore. They also tore off my chest elastoplast and discovered I was allergic to it. A pretty pink rash, I believe. I was slowly but surely joining the world of the living again. I was washed down again and happily recognised my pyjamas. It was easy to put the top on. But the size of the bandage on my thigh, where they had taken a skin graft—no way was the nurse going to get my jim jams over that. I asked the nurse if I could get out of bed and walk around to the other side.

She looked surprised, but she carefully manoeuvred the drip around to the left side of the bed. I sat up, swung my right leg over, and tried to move my left leg to join it, but the pain was excruciating. I realised I wasn't going to be able to walk for a while. But at least I had tried!

The nurse asked me if I would try and drink some water from a glass. She held the glass to my mouth but the water just poured out. Then we tried with a spoon. Same reaction. I couldn't suck either! I was unperturbed, but the nurse was determined she was going to get something down me. An ice-cream from the kitchen arrived. The nurse mashed it up and put a small amount on to the spoon. I tried to eat as I remembered, but nothing happened. We persevered and I managed to eat some of it, although quite a lot ended up on the bib down my front. Then the nurse had a bright idea: crushed ice. It was like small grains of glass on my tongue, but it did slowly go down.

I soon discovered that speaking was very difficult too. The sounds didn't come out the way I wanted and my voice was totally unfamiliar. This was obviously due to the obturator in my mouth. I remembered what Mr Issa had said about not being able to speak without it. It then dawned on me what the radiographer had meant about learning to speak again. I had lost half my palate, and although I had an artificial one, it was different from the original. I would just have to practice.

Some time later Dr De Silva, Mr Wallace's registrar, came into my room. I recognised his wild hairstyle! He smiled, asked how I was and told me he was going to take the packing out of my nose.

By this time I had developed a technique which took my mind away if something deeply unpleasant was happening to me. I would pretend I was on the golden sands of a beach in France, the sun beating down and the sounds of the sea in the distance. It worked for me and completely took my mind away from the dreadful facts of matter in hand.

Once he had gone Sister Brookes came in. 'Come on

Christine, you are coming back to Ward Eight. You have been here long enough.' Great excitement! One of the nurses wheeled my bed out of the room and another nurse wheeled the drip beside me. I waved goodbye and was pushed into a larger room, then into a corridor. We came out on to the main corridor leading to Ward Eight.

It was lovely to be back in my more familiar surroundings. Some of my flowers looked sad and jaded—rather like me I suppose. The ward nurses came in to see me and were full of smiles. I said how nice it was to be back with them, but what had they done to my flowers? Sister Brookes told me not to be so cheeky, they were over a week old. I asked what day it was.

'Wednesday, you have been in Intensive Care since Friday,' she told me.

The following days were filled with regular visits from the physiotherapist, who really put me through my paces. I suffered no discomfort from my face at all, just irritation at not being able to speak clearly and the most annoying condition of all was my nose, which never stopped running. I felt like one of the children at play school. The beastly thing was I couldn't feel my nose, it did not exist as far as I was concerned. It was only when a nurse came in and said, 'Oh dear Christine, your nose.' She would promptly get a tissue and wipe it for me.

I had X-rays of my chest—I suppose you could call it that, you definitely wouldn't call it a bust any more! I was most impressed with this portable machine and wondered why I was having X-rays. But nurses are very good at evading questions, and I was none the wiser for asking.

Mr Wallace came to see me, smiling, and obviously very pleased with my progress. The histology report (science of organic tissue) on the bone removed from my face was very good and as the tissue around the eye was not infected he had left it intact. The bone which supported the muscle holding the eye, however, had been removed, which made the eye droop. But the main thing was that the report was good and the bone was not badly diseased.

'Does that mean I'm cured?' I asked.

'Well, we never guarantee a hundred per cent cure, but I would say ninety-nine per cent.'

I felt like hugging him. I was delighted, and couldn't wait to tell Chris.

I was determined now to get up. My thigh, where they had taken the skin graft, was the most painful thing I could imagine. It itched and itched and I couldn't get to it! This was the one obstacle that kept me from getting out of bed, or so I thought. I had tried to stand up, but with the drip still attached this was difficult. Now the drip was removed and I was going to walk.

I asked the nurse if she would take me for a walk. She helped me to heave myself out of bed, all five stone of me and I stood up. It felt very strange, my knees wobbled under the strain as I hobbled the few steps to the door.

I must have looked like something out of a horror movie, or some bizarre comedy. The pain in my leg was excruciatingly painful. Then enough was enough and I gave in. But I returned triumphant.

The unpleasant thing about being immobile is the dependence on bed-pans. Jane, a very young nurse, helped me aboard on this occasion and I happened to look to my left. There for the first time I saw my reflection in the mirror. I couldn't believe it was me. I nodded my head to make sure. It was unrecognisable. What I could see of my face was red and swollen, and my upper lip looked as if I had been in a bundle with Mohammed Ali. It was grotesque.

Great excitement. I was going to have my stitches out. At last, I was going to have that ghastly bandage removed. I was surprised to see the doctor: she was very young and attractive—I had imagined someone much older. She worked silently and slowly as she began to remove the bandages. It was luxurious and I felt like having a good scratch but thought it unlady-like. I lay very flat as she removed the pad from over my left eye. It was very bright and felt rather uncomfortable and since I was unable to focus properly I closed my eyes. I didn't feel one single stitch removed. Sister Smith said how marvellous it was, and the nurses piled into the room to see. They were just a blur to me.

Chris was invited in to look and he said nothing he just smiled gently.

The next day there appeared familiar faces: Mr Issa, with John and Harry. As a maxillo-facial surgeon, Mr Issa had played a major role in my operation—as had the marvellous team of plastic surgeons who had also been present. He asked how I was and then proceeded to tell me he had come to remove the obturator to see if everything was all right. I wasn't at all concerned at first. I sat up and a bib was placed around my neck— now I know how children feel. By placing the bib around you, it makes you feel obliged to dribble or spit all over it—just to please them. The fight and tussle to loosen the wires around my teeth which held the obturator in place was unpleasant to say the least. It was impossible to describe the sensation I experienced as Mr Issa manoeuvred the offending object from my mouth.

Afterwards I spoke to Mr Issa but the sounds that came from my mouth were unrecognisable. The three faces looked at me, I don't know what they were thinking. A nurse wiped my mouth as I tried to swallow the swimming pool of saliva in my mouth, but instead I almost choked. I couldn't swallow: to swallow you push your tongue to the roof of your mouth. As there was only half a roof, it didn't work. I lay there bewildered at these sensations.

Mr Issa rinsed the obturator and examined it. To me it looked enormous and what's more I knew it had to be replaced. I wouldn't have been in Mr Issa's shoes for anything.

From that visit on, a new routine began in my life. After every meal I had to clean out my mouth with a solution of bicarbonate of soda. The first experience was quite hilarious. The nurse arrived armed with jug and hose and proceeded to show me how to do it. The first squeeze of the hose and the water poured from out of my mouth down my nose.

I imagined myself at a friend's house after dinner: Excuse me, whilst I go and hose out the bathroom. I managed to get puddles of water on the floor, as the drip ran down my arms. There must be an easier way than this, I thought.

Mummy and Daddy came to visit me. It was so lovely to see

them, though it must have been an awful shock for them to have seen me looking so ghastly. I asked them if they had brought my new potatoes and salmon. They laughed and we reminisced about my first visit to hospital when I was twelve. I had joined the boys' gym club at school and thought I could do what they could do. Well, I couldn't and ended up with a smashed elbow. I disliked the hospital food intensely, as I suppose most fussy twelve-year-olds would, and Mummy smuggled my favourite food in to me.

My parents were the first visitors I had had and I found it quite exhausting. I fought to keep my eyes open, but would waken and see their faces smiling. I began to feel sad, and wished I was twelve and they could take me home with them.

After they left, I walked out into the corridor where there was a huge arrangement of flowers in a large vase. They reminded me of my grandmother's garden, I hadn't seen flowers like them since then and I tried to sniff them. Another discovery, I couldn't smell. A lady came out of another side ward and said hello to me. I asked her about the flowers, and she said they were out of her garden, and were called Solomon's Seal. I told her of how they reminded me of my grandmother's garden, and what beautiful plants they were.

Lo and behold the following day she brought me a large plastic bag with some roots of the plant. That evening I gave them to Chris, with strict instructions for Mummy to plant them. Chris is very clever, but when it comes to gardening I'm afraid he is not really quite sure what he should be doing.

Two weeks after the operation Chris came and told me the most exciting news. I had seen a number of close friends during the past few days and had coped quite well, so on the next day, if I was very good, the children could come and see me.

I was up at six o'clock the next morning. By 'up' I mean, waiting for three o'clock to arrive. I didn't sleep at all well during my stay in hospital and refused sleeping tablets. I was so excited at seeing the children I couldn't wait for dawn to break and bring the day nearer to me.

The day of course was endless, and three o'clock seemed hours away. If I had been at home I would have mown the lawn, or found something worthwhile to do.

The sun was shining and it was going to be a hot day. Sister Brookes came to the rescue. 'Put on your shoes, I'm going to take you for a little walk.' I put on my dressing gown and slippers, bunged my pockets full of tissues, Sister took my arm and we set off. We walked out into the garden and down the steps. Past the children's ward and on into a large open area, rather like a field. In the middle was a lake, and we walked around the lake. How my legs ached! When we arrived home I collapsed on the bed and slept. I'm still not sure if Sister Brookes' intentions were all together for my benefit or for the nurses! I would have been impossible waiting for the afternoon to come.

At long last, I heard Chris's footsteps coming down the corridor. I stood by my bed, but I couldn't wait and rushed to the door. He was alone! I stamped my feet in rage. 'Where are they? You promised, you promised.' I clung to his arms and wept.

'Calm down. They are here. I left them in the waiting area, before I brought them in. I thought I had better check that you were all right.' It took me a few minutes to calm down, dry my eyes and compose myself. I climbed on top of the bed and rested against the pillows.

'Please fetch them, darling, I'm all right now.'

Dominic was the first to come in, followed by Matthew then Claire. They stood at the bottom of the bed, their faces looking so apprehensive, not wanting to show any worries at seeing me.

'Hello, my darlings, I have missed you!' I held my arms out and Dominic leapt on to the bed and hugged me.

He looked closely at my face and said, 'Oh blue stitches, my favourite colour.' I burst out laughing and asked him what he meant. 'Your stitches, Mummy, they are blue, you do look lovely.'

The ice was broken and the three of them cuddled me all at once. Their presence was intoxicating and I was filled with love.

Life to me was like one great big jig-saw puzzle. Chris was the biggest and most important part, and surrounding him to complete the puzzle were the children. Our family add to the pattern and friends form the background; the pattern growing with additional friends. I was never so aware of this as I was at that moment, and I felt complete.

As long as I had the stitches in my face, I knew I wouldn't be going home. Once they were removed, there would be no holding me.

One day Sister Brookes appeared, 'Come on Christine, we're going for another walk.'

'Oh no, not to the lake again.'

'No, down to the Plastic Surgery Ward to see if they will take your stitches out.'

Elation! We walked along the corridor, past Intensive Care and on along the corridor to the Plastics Ward. We stood outside the Sister's office. She was very young, tiny and super-efficient. She ignored us and answered the telephone. She then proceeded to administer orders to other junior nurses. Our presence seemed totally irrelevant to her, and she continued to ignore us.

Eventually, Sister Brookes spoke to her. She explained that the doctor who had done my stitches had advised that I should be brought down to Plastics to have them removed.

The outburst that followed amazed me. The gist of it was that nobody ever told her anything, she wasn't going to do it, she was far too busy with her patients, it just couldn't be done and a few more exasperated sentences.

I stood there and looked at her with my one eye. I wanted to tell her where she could stuff her plastic surgery ward and that she was totally unthinking and unfeeling.

But I didn't. I still wish I had.

Sister Brookes was a true professional. 'I'll phone you,' she said, and we walked back. Sister Brookes said, 'She isn't usually like that, she's probably very busy and rushed off her feet.'

The following morning, Sister Brookes and I went back down and were greeted by a different, very confident nurse. I was led into a room with a tilted stretcher-type bed. I looked around and it seemed that everywhere I looked was stainless steel, even the walls. It was comforting to have Sister Brookes at my side as the nurse removed my eyepad. 'You'll be in here again I expect, having more surgery for your eye and lip,' she said.

This idea had never occurred to me, and as she deftly removed the beautiful blue stitches I wondered what she meant.

The following day, Mr Wallace came to see me.

'Please Mr Wallace, when can I go home?' It was the week of the Jubilee and the children were going to a street party. I did so want to go home, but I still had a sore throat. I tried gargling—it was like poison. But later that day, when Mr Wallace asked how my throat was, I told him: 'Cured, fantastic stuff, one gargle and you're cured or poisoned.'

'All right. Perhaps we will let you go home on Friday.' It was like music in my ears. Chris wouldn't believe me when I said Mr Wallace had said I could go home. He thought I was teasing. As if I would!

The great day came and Chris arrived with my clothes. He had brought my smallest pair of trousers, skirt and sweater. It was quite alarming, even my stretch pants looked baggy, the bra was superfluous and I needed a belt to hold the trousers up! Armed with a bag full of eyepads, tape, jug and hose I headed for Sister's office. Saying thank you seemed much too empty. I hadn't the vocabulary to say how we both felt.

We walked down the familiar corridor and I stopped outside Intensive Care. 'I want to go in and thank them and say goodbye,' I said.

I couldn't speak, I just kissed them and muttered, 'Thank you'. I turned away, and then, as we walked to the door I said, 'Oh, by the way, have you a thirty-four-inch bust anywhere? I had one when I came in, but I seem to have lost it somewhere.'

The looks on their faces were priceless.

Chapter Seven

The route home was so familiar. The way I was absorbing everything my good eye could see made me feel I had been away for three years, not three weeks. Windsor Great Park looks regal at any time of the year, but that early summer it looked wonderful. Everywhere was so beautifully green: the huge oaks were bursting with leaves and life was so abundantly obvious. I promised myself a walk there as soon as I was well enough.

I wondered if the children would be home from school. As the car entered our road I could see a crowd of people, mainly children, standing at the corner. My heart missed a beat, I felt dreadfully embarrassed and wanted to hide somewhere. As the car turned right, I recognised two familiar faces, looking full of excitement. Chris stopped the car.

'We'll come and see you in a minute, Mummy. Denise has phoned the fire brigade—that house is on fire. Isn't it super, we're waiting for the fire engine.'

Oh dear, what an anti-climax to my homecoming! But, after all, it's not often one sees a fire engine at the bottom of the street, is it?

Chris helped me out of the car and I heard a scream: 'Mummy!' Claire flung herself around my neck and kissed me. Not long after my arrival, the boys rushed in.

'There's three fire engines now. They rescued the rabbit and the baby. It's ever so exciting!'

'Whose baby and whose rabbit?' I asked.

'Candy's. Her Mum was out and there was a big explosion, but nobody's hurt—and the rabbit's all right too.'

I never did hear truly what happened, but it was a wonderful distraction for the boys and it did allow Claire and me five minutes together.

It was luxurious to sleep in my own bed again. Even more so than when we returned from a three-week holiday in France. We had slept on lilos in an awning attached to our friends' caravan. Having gone barefoot for most of the time, my feet were like sandpaper and would catch on the sleeping bag. It was awful! On returning home and sleeping in my own bed, I vowed I would never experience the same sensation again. Yet, here I was, luxuriating in sipping tea in my own bed and assuring myself that there was nothing like your own sheets and pillows.

Chris wouldn't be pleased about the pillow slips though. Every day in hospital I had the pillow slips changed, as my nose and mouth took on the nature of dripping taps all night. (All day too but I was more in control during the day time.) Never mind, three cheers for the washing machine and Mummy.

The next day was Saturday, a very special one too. For today was the day of the children's Jubilee party. I sat and looked out of the front window and enjoyed watching the preparations for the party. Even Chris, who is very quiet and undemonstrative, hung an enormous Union Jack from our bedroom window. The children helped to decorate all the houses and gardens in the road with flags and streamers. The transformation was a lovely sight to see. Then the caretaker from the school arrived with a lorry laden with tables and chairs. Everyone was so busy helping set them out, they all looked most organised and proficient.

I slept for most of the afternoon, but was awakened by the boys giggling, obviously getting ready for the tea. It was a very happy scene and I loved just looking on. I felt so grateful to be there and thankful for the memory of such a united day.

Mummy arrived on Sunday evening in order to look after me whilst Chris went to work. This became the pattern for the next few months. Daddy would collect her on a Friday evening and poor Mum spent her weekends catching up on her housework and leaving Daddy prepared for the following week. I don't know how she coped and remained so cheerful.

We would spend much of the day chatting and reminiscing, as mothers and daughters will do. Chris did all the shopping and cooked the evening meal. Sometimes Mummy would prepare it, but it was rather different cooking the sort of dinner that six people required, compared to the evening meal she and Daddy had.

I didn't seem to fit in at all. The children were completely organised by Chris for their morning routine. I began to feel superfluous and started to become withdrawn. I didn't want to see anyone and wouldn't even answer the telephone.

Dr Perry visited me, he looked at my eye and the inside of my mouth and throat. Mr Wallace had sent him a detailed report on everything that had been done. I explained to Dr Perry about the sensations I was experiencing. He encouraged me to be patient and take my own time. Easier said than done.

The weather was warm enough to sit outside and in the seclusion of the garden I felt secure. Janette was once again planning to take the children away for the weekend. To give Chris and me time together.

I hadn't seen her since my visit to hospital and I was apprehensive at the meeting. Chris had the children's clothes all organised, Claire had her camera and Matthew was hunting down the wellies. When Janette's car pulled up I hugged the children and wished them a happy weekend. I didn't want them to go and ran upstairs, not wanting the children to see my tears. I heard Janette's voice, with its familiar Scottish sharpness.

'Good. Are ye all ready?' I knew I couldn't let them go without saying goodbye to her. Hurriedly, I walked down the stairs. Janette's eyes met mine. 'Hello there, how are you?' she said.

The lump rose in my throat and I fled back up to my room. Why was I feeling like this? I felt so mean. So as I watched them climb into the car and wave, I lifted the curtain and waved back frantically.

But the same thing happened later that day, when Ray, one of our best friends, came walking down the pathway to the front door.

'Please, please don't let him in, I don't want to see him,' I said, hiding behind the lounge door, terrified.

Ray didn't even knock. He had left a small parcel for me at

the door. Chris picked it up and gave it to me. Inside was a minute arrangement of orange crocuses, encased in an oval glass dome. It was so beautiful and so typical of Ray and Mary. They were the dearest friends and understood how I felt.

Chris was always so patient with me, he never once questioned my behaviour or made me feel foolish. I couldn't understand why this great fear of seeing people had taken over. The people I seemed to dread the most were the ones I held most dear, our closest friends.

The following week I went to visit Mr Wallace. I had a long wait in the clinic waiting room, and was feeling very low and despondent. Eventually my turn came and in I went.

I explained how I had been reacting to meeting people. Apparently this was not at all unusual—they had expected this reaction when I was in hospital. In my case it was just a little delayed.

'There are some tablets I can prescribe for you, which will help.' Mr Wallace said.

'No thank you, I don't want them.'

'But you need only take them for a few weeks,' he said.

'I don't want any tablets, thank you. I'll cope with it on my own in my own way,' I said firmly. 'If my body can possibly cope on its own, then it is much better for it to do so.'

I was—and still am—a great believer of 'mind over matter', and was determined to try and come to terms with my face, as this was very obviously the problem, in my own way. I really had to accept people as I had done before. I knew my face was horribly scarred, although nobody knew what my eye was like, as I hid this behind the eyepad. If I tried to eat more and get stronger, I was sure I could cope.

My visit to Mr Issa was the next important event on the calendar. I wasn't looking forward to having the obturator removed at all, but he was charming as usual, and I began to relax. Mr Issa then proceeded to remove the obturator and to clean out the inside of my mouth and cheek with a suction pipe, which was not at all pleasant. After the obturator was replaced and I could speak again, Mr Issa said, 'Now it's your turn. I want you to try and remove it yourself.' He showed me how to fit

57

the metal clip under my nail and pull down. This loosened the obturator so it dropped into my mouth and made me retch and feel violently sick. A swift movement from Mr Issa and it was out.

I was told to practice for a while, until I felt pretty confident. Confident! It was like driving a double-decker bus into our garage!

Mr Issa's final advice was to remove and scrub the prosthesis, as he now called it, three times a day and to scrub my teeth and hose out my mouth.

That evening, as we sat eating and chatting about school and football, I suddenly realised that after our meal I had to clean my obturator and my mouth and I was on my own! I tried to stay calm and, not concentrating, sipped my orange—and it came pouring down my nose! I had forgotten to keep my head up. The children roared with laughter—I didn't think it was that funny.

Afterwards I locked the bathroom door, took a deep breath and aimed for the washbasin. I carefully measured one teaspoonful of bicarbonate of soda into the two-pint jug and added warm water. My receiver (posh name for bowl) was a plastic margarine tub—a pretty one with pink flowers. I remembered the procedure exactly as Mr Issa had told me: 'Fill the basin with water, then if you should drop the obturator it won't break, but land in the water.' This I did. I looked at my unfamiliar face in the mirror, and said, 'Here goes.'

I couldn't get it out. I eased it, I pulled it, it came unstuck and lay on my tongue like a visitor from outer space. How *was* I going to get it out? At last I forced it through my lips, tearing the corners and making them bleed. I stared at the object in my hand and then scrubbed it, scrubbed my teeth and hosed out my mouth and cheek with the bicarbonate mixture. At this moment I wasn't feeling too confident as with great difficulty I had removed my 'mouth', but now I had to replace it. Carefully I rinsed it under the tap and tried to raise it to my mouth. It wouldn't come. Oh God! The chain to the plug had become attached to one of the metal hooks. I couldn't believe it, it could only happen to me! I fiddled about with it, but it wouldn't come off. I couldn't shout for Chris, as without my 'mouth' I couldn't speak, let alone shout; besides I wasn't going to let him see me without my teeth! Patience and a little prayer and at last it became unhooked. I was hot all over and shaking, as I weakly sank on to the side of the bath.

Deep breath, remember what Mr Issa had said. I couldn't remember anything. It just wouldn't fit in the gap between my teeth. Try it at an angle, then. I fiddled and pushed, and eventually it returned home.

Three times a day! As I lay in bed that night I thought about it. How can I go through the rest of my life having to perform that task three times a day? Is my nose going to run for ever? Will I dribble and have to have a clean pillow slip every day—*forever*?

I was going to have to muster every grain of courage I had to get back to normal and to face my friends and start living again.

Chapter Eight

Poor Chris. Saturdays were not the same any more. He was endlessly loading the washing machine up with school uniforms or, while Claire was left at home to supervise me and answer the telephone, he was off to the supermarket with the boys. I felt I had to show him that I was working hard too, at getting better and learning to face the world. So one afternoon I suggested that we go along to a nearby school fete. I thought it would be a good way of meeting people again, and as it wasn't my own children's school and I wouldn't know too many people, I could stay relatively anonymous.

Chris was delighted that I wanted to go and wrapped me up as if it were winter, with a scarf wrapped round my thin head of hair. It was a dull day, very cool, and not really the sort of day for a summer fete at all.

We walked very slowly towards the school. My legs felt strange, partly due to lack of use and partly because my shoes felt too large. I hadn't realised that when one lost weight, it went from all over. I felt very cold and shivery.

As we entered the school and saw all the people, I wanted to run away and hide but I held tightly on to Chris's arm as we walked on towards the field. I recognised two of the teachers, but they didn't see me.

'It's Auntie Chris, it's Auntie Chris, Mummy, Mummy, look!' I recognised the voice and looked over to my left and there was Rebecca, the most adorable four-year-old from play school. A large lump rose in my throat and I couldn't speak. We walked on, and coming towards us across the field was Kenneth, Janette's husband. I couldn't look at him, let alone speak, so I turned around trying hard not to cry out loud when Lisa, a little girl from next door, came rushing up with a cactus in a plastic cup. 'Here you are, Auntie Chris, it's for you.'

I took the plant and looked at her smiling face. 'Thank you Lisa, that's very sweet of you.' Then she was gone. 'Let's go home Chris.' People waved and smiled. 'Nice to see you,' they called. 'Take care.' But I was like ice, my hands were blue and I felt so empty inside. As soon as we got back Chris put me to bed.

When I woke up I felt better. Even though my feelings were mixed up, and I couldn't understand why I felt so nervous, when everyone was so very friendly, I did have a smug feeling of, well I did it. I have gone out and faced people. Not very well, but I had done it.

As time went on I felt that I was on the way to recovery. The days were filled with obturator washing, eye bathing and face creaming, and my leg, where they took the skin for the graft, was a terrible irritation. It kept me awake at night itching and, most inconvenient of all, when I had plastered it with cream I couldn't wear tights or trousers. I tried tying a piece of white lint over it, but this would fall down around my ankle—not a pretty sight.

But I was going out more—even accepting an invitation to dinner with some old friends—something I could never have done only a few weeks before. It took me ages to decide what to wear but in the end I chose a long-sleeved blouse and a long skirt. I took great care making up my one eye and I felt pleased with the result. I must remember to keep my head up when I drink, I thought, and Chris promised to tell me if my nose needed wiping.

It was lovely to see our friends again, and I didn't disgrace myself. I just missed my plate with the peas, and dear Chris dived under the table for me and rescued them. We had a delicious meal—I even tackled the melon, but had to give up on the biscuits and cheese. I tried, but I hadn't trained my teeth to bite yet!

It was that night that I decided that it was over: I felt I could

61

speak and meet anyone now without feeling that ghastly sensation of panic. I hoped now my depression had gone forever.

By this time I was finding it impossible to read. When I put on my reading glasses they squashed my eyepad into my eye, making it very sore and uncomfortable.

Dear Mr Wallace, with an answer for everything, suggested a monocle, but I would have to be very refined, no more cockney accents. On one visit I had told him that it was so much easier to speak badly, without finishing off the ends of my words. I still had to concentrate when speaking and remember to slow down or else it came out like mumbo-jumbo.

It was great fun trying to use the monocle, it took a lot of practice holding it in. As you can imagine, everyone had a try. It was rather a hazard though. It tended to get in the way: it dangled in the washing-up, it hung in the food mixer and even got shut in the loo! It gave us all a lot of amusement and best of all I could see to read.

Hair wash day. Chris managed to wash everywhere else besides my hair, but it saved me using up my precious energy doing it myself.

I held a towel tightly over my face, covering the eyepad, while Chris lathered away. He was unusually quiet and very gentle, but eventually he said, 'Look at your hair.' I took the towel away from my eyes and in the bottom of the bath was my hair, floating in the water. The plug was so blocked with hair the water couldn't run away.

I stared in horror. Chris's hands were covered in hair too. I wrapped the towel around my head and sat down in front of the dressing table. I gently patted my hair dry, removed the towel and started gently to comb it. Handfuls came out. By the time I had combed it all, the hair was piled in mounds around my shoulders. I looked in the mirror. This was really more than I could bear. I had coped with the bald patch behind my left ear, but this was all over my head. I couldn't contain myself any longer, the deep grief I felt exploded inside me and I cried and cried, inconsolable.

*

Another problem arose at this time, my mother was looking increasingly tired. It had been an enormous strain on her, coping with our demanding family, and, most of all, the shock that her own daughter had cancer.

It was almost the end of the summer term, and the children were finishing school on Friday. I discussed with Chris the possibility of Mummy going home for a week to see how I could cope. He thought if I felt well enough we would give it a try and if it failed, my mother would come back.

The Saturday morning came, and it was time for me to say goodbye to Mummy. I just hugged her in my arms, the words wouldn't come, I just wasn't going to cry! We stood there in the kitchen holding each other.

'I love you, Mummy.' She let go and walked away. The children were kissing her and shouting goodbye. I sat in the lounge, on my own.

We soon became organised, and Claire, who was coming up to her thirteenth birthday, was terrific. She even washed the kitchen floor. Dominic cleaned the bathroom—and the walls and the ceiling! Matthew helped clear away and wash up. Chris was very proficient at cooking now. His entire Sunday morning was taken up with preparation of the Sunday feast. That weekend we had roast chicken and roast potatoes with stuffing and bread sauce. He paraded the chicken into the dining room as if he had given birth to it! It did make me smile, as the children told me he was wonderful. And rice pudding for dessert. This was too much—he was becoming a threat to my popularity!

'I don't know how you did it,' he said that evening. 'All the things you did during the week, entertaining friends, cooking Sunday lunch and finding time to share with us in between. I never realised what hard work it was and how much you had to do.'

'That's just being a housewife dear,' I replied, demurely. 'And you forgot to mention mowing the lawn, doing the garden, washing my car and making my clothes and Claire's.'

I think I'd made my point.

*

At last there was something I was really looking forward to: Dominic's school sports day. It was a lovely hot July day, but I was dressed up for winter. I had gained some weight, but I was still very thin, and completely bald on the back of my head, where the radiation had penetrated. But none of that mattered. We shouted and cheered the children on with whistles and encouragement from all four corners of the field. Dominic ran in an obstacle race, where the children had to put on a raincoat, hat, and a pair of wellington boots, and then run to the finishing rope carrying a huge umbrella. They all looked so small and adorable. I was so excited because Dominic streaked ahead and won the race. He looked so happy, especially as we were all there to see him.

An announcement came over the speaker. 'Come on, mothers, it's your turn now.' As the mums lined up, miles away down the field, a voice behind me said, 'Come on, Mrs Piff. You won last year.'

I looked down, and there stood Jay, a tall eight-year-old, one of my footballers. Slightly taken aback, I hesitated a moment and then said, 'I'm giving someone else a chance this year, Jay. I'll try again next year.'

Next was the father's race. There were so many of them, and they all seemed keener to win than their children. Their faces were set in grim determination, and as they passed me it sounded like a herd of buffalo. They were nearly at the finishing line when two fell, including my great friend, Terry! I couldn't believe my eyes as he took off, flew upwards in the air, dived over the rope and skidded down on his chest with his legs in the air, gliding along on his stomach.

I began to laugh and laugh. I couldn't stop. It was the funniest thing I had seen for years. My stomach ached, my cheek hurt, and I was crying with laughter.

Terry walked towards us, a huge grin on his face, with mudstains all over his knees and on the front of his sweater. He had grass embedded in his watchstrap. We tried to contain ourselves and muffle our sniggers. 'The spirit is willing, but the flesh is weak,' he said, ruefully, as he collapsed in a chair.

It had been the most enjoyable day. My fears of meeting people were at last fading. It took a lot of effort, but I was learning to face the outside world. Though I still needed to sleep during the day to recharge my batteries, and my days were spent sitting talking to friends or day dreaming, I felt myself picking up the threads of my life again. The fact that I was willing to do that was the most important step I could take.

Chapter Nine

In September I had another appointment with Mr Wallace. I was looking forward to seeing him: I was feeling so much better and had gained weight. It's amazing what the sun can do for one's morale.

Mr Wallace examined my mouth and cleaned my cheek from inside. It had been a few weeks since I had received proper treatment and Mr Wallace seemed to be taking extra care. He put down his instrument and pushed back his chair.

'I need to clean your mouth more thoroughly,' he said. 'Under an anaesthetic, so it will mean you coming in for a couple of days. Can you come in on the fourteenth?'

'Yes, of course,' I answered automatically.

On the way home I said to Chris, 'How horrid to have to have another anaesthetic.' Chris agreed, but added, 'Never mind, it's only for a short time and you will only be away a few days.'

On the fourteenth, we dropped the children off at school, and immediately drove to Wexham Park Hospital. Not a private little room this time—Sister Smith had given me my old bed back. As I unpacked my things, I remembered my first visit, back in February: what a lot of water had run under the bridge since then.

The usual pattern followed. I was handed the jug for a sample. I duly performed and wrote on the brown paper bag, Neat Champagne, and left it with the others.

After the pre-med injection I had to part with my obturator. This made me feel very uncomfortable, as I dribbled and lay there trying hard to sleep.

66

The porter arrived with Sister Smith and off I went, along the familiar corridor and into the doors marked Theatre.

'Hallo, Christine,' said a voice. It was Mr Wallace, dressed in green, wearing a hat and mask. I wanted to speak, but no words came. Hearing his voice I felt safe, and I could remember no more.

There was no discomfort when I came round, no unfamiliar bandages when my hands explored my face. The familiar eyepad was still there. A nurse helped me sit up and handed me my obturator. I sipped some water, feeling rather sick.

Everyone seemed subdued and not their bright breezy selves. I was glad when Sister Smith said I could go home. We spent a quiet weekend: I was still very sleepy, and having the anaesthetic had made me take a step backwards in progress and it showed.

A week later I was in hospital. I had taken great care in cleaning my mouth every time I had eaten, making sure Mr Wallace's care was not neglected by me. I hoped everything would be fine.

We sat outside the familiar door. The same picture stared at us from the wall: a tiger cub in long grass staring at an enormous grasshopper. At last, 'Would you come in, Christine?'

I took my seat in front of Mr Wallace and Chris sat behind me against the wall.

'Not good news, I'm afraid.' I stared back at him, unable to believe my ears. 'The result of the biopsy shows another tumour has grown behind your eye.' I sat there, not moving, not saying anything. I felt hollow inside.

'I haven't decided what to do yet. I must discuss the problem with my colleagues. Please would you come to Dr Strickland's clinic on Tuesday.'

I felt Chris take my arm. It was if I had fallen off the world and was floating in limbo. Chris took me to the car and helped me into the seat. He said nothing. We drove home in silence. There was nothing to say.

I can't remember preparing or eating supper. I spoke to the children, but I wasn't really there. I was standing at the sink washing up, and there was a loud knock at the door. Chris answered it. It was Albert Fothergill, his boss. Albert came into the kitchen and chatted and smiled. Chris finally told him about the results of the biopsy.

He looked at me and said, 'I think you are marvellous, you are the bravest person I know.' He took my hand and said goodbye. Chris and he went into the hall. I heard the door shut and Chris went into the lounge to the children.

I dried my hands and automatically applied my hand cream. I leant against the cupboard, massaging the smooth cream in. I was still stunned, there was a barrier around me that nobody could penetrate, I was completely and absolutely on my own.

I went upstairs to the bathroom, the only place where I could lock myself away. I sat on the edge of the bath. How can this be true? How can it be? I was doing so well. What have I done wrong that this can happen to us? I looked down and on the bathroom floor were Dominic's school shoes. I took a deep breath and bent and picked them up. He knows he shouldn't leave them there! I stopped surprised at my own reaction. I looked at the small shoes in my hand and buried my face in them. Oh God. I don't want to die, please, *please* don't let me die. I'm needed too much, they couldn't cope without me. I cried and cried, pleading with God to spare me.

That night as I lay in Chris's arms, our whole lives threatened by this traumatic shock, I tried to find words to speak to him. I couldn't; the thought of me dying and leaving him and the children on their own was more than I could bear. The same thoughts I knew were going through his mind and neither of us could speak a word.

I loved him so much, more than mere words could explain, the thought of not sharing the rest of his life with him was worse than any physical torture. Not to be with the children any more, not to be there to help Claire grow into a woman, to share her joys and her sorrows. Matthew—how would he take my dying? He needed me so much, he always wanted me with him, and would say, 'I wish I could magic you small and put you in my pocket.' Little Dominic, he was my sunshine on a rainy day. He was the youngest, would it be easier for him or not?

After a while, a composure came over me. I had let my

emotions tear me apart and now I had to be in control. I felt cheated and angry at the cancer returning, but I wouldn't be beaten by it. After all, Mr Wallace hadn't said that I was going to die and I wouldn't. I would fight, and fight. No cancer was going to steal my life away from me, not without a battle anyway.

The phone rang the next morning and my heart missed a beat. I didn't want to have to share my agony with any of my friends. Instead it was the informal voice of a receptionist. 'Mr Wallace has made an appointment for you to see Professor Harrison at the Royal National Throat, Nose and Ear Hospital, Grays Inn Road, next Tuesday.'

How I lived through those four days I don't know. I just couldn't admit to the children that another tumour had grown. I was so proud of the way they had shared in my illness and understood about cancer. It was too much to expect them to share any more anguish and worry. Instead I told them I was going to see a doctor who might help sort out the problem of my eye.

The journey through London seemed endless. I was grateful for the radio in the car, it helped distract us from the matter in hand. Would Professor Harrison be able to do anything? I had never felt so low or so sad in my entire life.

The waiting for Professor Harrison was like a nightmare, only Chris's hand gave me comfort. It was all so unfamiliar, I felt like a foreigner in a different world. I was ice cold, my hands shook and were damp with perspiration.

A nurse came up to me. 'Mrs Piff?' I stood up and we followed her along the maze of corridors until we came to a door. I followed the nurse in. Professor Harrison stood up, smiling and shook my hand.

'Now tell me all about it,' he said kindly.

I seemed to ramble on about the past nine months, until my visit today.

'You have three children?'

'Yes. Claire, Matthew and Dominic.' I explained that they knew about my illness, but not about this second tumour.

'You have a lot to live for, Mrs Piff. Mr Wallace tells me of the great support your husband has been to you during this time.' He was silent for a while. 'Well now, don't despair. I can operate, but you must pay for your future. It means a drastic operation, removing your eye and all the muscle and tissue behind it.'

I wanted to jump up and dance! The joy and relief I felt were immense. This wonderful man was giving me back my future. I don't know if he realised how much this meant to us.

He went on to explain about the operation. Cancer of the sinus was very rare and a maxillectomy was performed. Unfortunately, in my case a group of cells had moved house and set up on their own. This called for more severe surgery to ensure that everything was removed. I didn't care. They could have whatever they wanted as long as I was still alive.

Professor Harrison put his arm around my shoulders. 'Come back in on Monday and we will fix you up. We'll need to fatten you up too by the feel of things!'

Chris and I fairly skipped to the car, we were so happy. You would have thought we had won a million pounds, but it was much more than that. It was life and hope. During the past few days we had both climbed an insurmountable obstacle and today had reached the peak. It didn't matter about tomorrow, for today we had hope.

Once more, a week of preparation. Filling the freezer with prepared meals and baking the children's favourite chocolate cake. It wasn't until a long time later that they confessed to me that it was the worst chocolate cake I had made. But they spread jam on it and declared it delicious!

I was so bitterly disappointed at the tumour recurring that I couldn't bring myself to tell the children the truth. They had fought with me all the way and to them I had come through and was recovering. To tell them that the cancer had returned seemed to cheat them of their courage and I couldn't bear to let them be as disappointed as I was. So, I told a little white lie. I told them that Professor Harrison was a very special doctor and he was going to have a look at my face and eye to see if Mr Wallace had done it properly. I said that Professor Harrison had taught Mr Wallace all he knew, and he was going to advise us on what could be done for my eye.

We joked about it, and I can remember Matthew saying, 'I hope Mr Wallace has done it properly, or else Professor Harrison will tell him off!'

Monday morning. As usual I went in the car with the children. The boys were fine though Claire was very quiet. But she gave me a broad smile and abruptly turned her back.

The journey to the Royal National was very dull. My tummy began to turn over, I never felt this way when I went to Wexham Park! I felt like a child must feel when being taken to boarding school for the first time. I remember thinking, if this is how they feel, I will never, never send my children away.

The Royal National is an old hospital in London—very dark and gloomy. Chris's arm was reassuring—he must have felt terrible too. We found the ward, a long, wide ward with six beds on one side, two beds at the end and on the opposite side two beds and then two intensive care beds. Both separate individual cubicles. My heart skipped a beat, as the nurse showed me to my bed. I was amongst the row of six.

I took off my clothes and put on my nightdress and dressing gown. I felt very cold. Chris and I sat side by side in the corridor, not speaking. Eventually I was invited into the examination room. I had a long chat to the doctor and he stared in disbelief at my positive attitude. When he explained that when they removed my eye it would be used for a cornea transplant I said I thought this was wonderful.

'My loss is someone else's gain; that is really good news.'

The doctor looked absolutely astonished. 'Mrs Piff,' he said, 'where do you get this happy attitude to life when you are undergoing such an ordeal?'

Chris answered for me. 'Christine always sees life through rose-coloured spectacles, and so, I'm sure, will the person who receives her eye.'

71

Chapter Ten

As I came round after the anaesthetic I felt completely disoriented. The nurses' faces were unfamiliar and so were the surroundings. But it didn't take long for my mind to adjust and I remembered where I was. I dozed the day away and awoke to find Chris holding my hand. I hoped I would feel as comfortable as this in two days' time, after the big operation.

I spent the next day writing letters and chatting to other patients. I was looking through a *Vogue* fashion magazine with a sweet girl who had undergone surgery for cancer of the larynx. Her voice was very soft, like a whisper and, the fool I was, I whispered back to her.

'I'm not hearing what you are saying, stupid,' she said. 'You don't have to whisper to me, because I whisper to you!' We both giggled like schoolgirls at each other and shared our histories.

One of the staff nurses came to see me and asked if I had a maxillectomy.

'Yes, Mr Wallace performed the operation at Wexham Park,' I told her.

'It is the neatest scar I have seen. Your mouth and upper lip are remarkable. How long ago did you have it done?'

'Four months,' I replied.

'You're a very lucky girl. Your obturator is beautiful, I have never seen such a neat one.'

I felt over the moon. I was so proud of Mr Wallace and Mr Issa. You would have thought the nurse was discussing the crown jewels, not my palate and false teeth! I wrote to them both to tell them about the praise. Then I felt very sad. I was out of their hands now, with strangers to take care of me. I felt a little uneasy. It was that child in me coming out again! No room for self-pity, fight the good fight and trust in the Lord and Professor Harrison.

Again I had the sheer luxury of hospital baths. The depth and length was remarkable—full of silky soft water. This was one of the few things that hadn't changed during the past months of my illness. No matter how ill I felt, when I climbed into a bath it was always glorious. A cup of tea never changed either. It still tasted as good.

Well, tonight, on the eve of my operation, I was enjoying my bath and thinking of the past months. Now that I had said goodbye to Chris, there was just one more goodbye I had to say. I looked at my face in the steamy mirror and removed the eyepad. I looked at my poor old eye. It was dull and sad, and rather crooked.

'Goodbye eye. Thanks for everything, be a good cornea for your new owner.'

I replaced the eyepad, knowing that I wouldn't see my eye again. Yet I was so happy. Believe it or not, I felt really excited. I didn't mind losing my eye at all, for I knew behind it lay the deadly tumour, and the sooner it went the better I would be.

A loud crash awoke me. My bed moved, and there was the sound of nurses hurrying and agitated voices. I strained to open my eye. My hands went up to my head. The eyepad was there. No other bandages. It was all over, and I was here. I pulled my head from the pillows and saw two nurses rushing out of my room pushing a large machine. I fell back to sleep, only to be awakened again by anxious voices, and the sound of people hurrying. Then I slept for ages. A nurse's voice disturbed my dreams.

'Good morning, Christine, time to have a wash.'

I sat up and couldn't believe it was all over. I couldn't feel my head or my face, but everywhere else felt good. I asked the nurse about the commotion during the night, had it really happened or had I imagined it?

'No, a patient was very ill and they required the resuscitator that was by your bed.'

'Is she all right?' I asked.

The young nurse's head hung low and she said, 'No, I'm afraid she died.'

I said nothing. Familiar faces walked past the windows in the ward and smiled at me. They were not allowed into my little glass cage, but I could whisper out to them.

A few days later the nurses moved me out of the intensive care room and I was put into another room. The sister removed my obturator and cleaned my mouth. She proceeded to give me a lecture on cleaning it. I was too tired and weary to be rude. It did cross my mind to tell her I couldn't stand up yet, but I didn't. She reminded me of a school matron.

Professor Harrison came in to see me. He looked at my eye—or where my eye had been.

'How does it look?' I asked.

'See for yourself,' he said. He helped me out of bed and I wobbled to the washbasin. There was a mirror above it. I took a deep breath and looked. My left eye looked closed and the eyelid was covered with gentian violet, a deep purple. There were no other scars on my face at all other than Mr Wallace's.

'It looks better than it did before, when it was open. At least it isn't lop-sided.'

He helped me back into bed. I was so grateful to him and thanked him profusely.

I slept soundly until Chris arrived. The children came to see me on the Sunday afternoon. I was thrilled to see them so bright and happy. They had enjoyed the drive to London and Chris had promised them a treat.

The visit didn't last long and I promised to be home by next Sunday. All I seemed to do was sleep, no doubt due to the drugs they were giving me. It was no use protesting here as I did in Wexham Park. I felt so weak that for once I just did as I was told.

On the Wednesday evening my parents came to see me. They had brought along an old friend of mine, whom I hadn't seen for years. Julia had lived next door to me when I was a child and lived in Stone in Staffordshire. We really went through childhood hating each other as far as I can remember! Julia was six months older than I, and she was taller, prettier and generally much cleverer than I was.

I can remember us playing together in our back yard. I was icing a house brick with chocolate-brown mud and I decorated it with the most beautiful heads of bright yellow buttercups. I can see it now, I was so delighted with it—and then Julia stamped on it! I think that was the final straw for me. I played with Pat, her younger sister, from then on. For the rest of the summer I walked around in rag bandages because Pat wanted to be a nurse, and I was her patient.

I hadn't seen Julia for many years, and it was lovely to reminisce about all the terrible things we used to get up to, and how I always seemed to get the blame and the good hidings. I had more good hidings than hot dinners in those days. Although my mother is only five feet, she made my bottom so sore I couldn't sit on it!

After Julia had left I thought about my childhood and wished I could borrow just a day from way back, when the sun always shone, the air was filled with the perfume of the hawthorn, and I could make mud pies and pick buttercups.

'Up you get, Christine, I'm going to wash your hair.'

The cheerful nurse succeeded in nearly drowning me! Well, not quite, but I was rather wet. It was fun though, and she took such care in brushing it dry for me. It did make me feel better having clean hair, but I was still exhausted, and all I did was sleep. When I awoke, Sister came to see me and said I could go home the next day, Saturday.

I couldn't wait to tell Chris. He didn't seem overjoyed. 'Are you sure you're all right?' he asked anxiously.

Excited goodbyes, and I couldn't wait. I saw the doctor in the morning. He gave all the details of future appointments to the sister and he wished me luck.

Chris arrived with Claire, Matthew and Dominic. I was beginning to feel awful, and wanted to escape as fast as possible. A nurse came and took my suitcase, Chris had his arms around me and we walked to the door.

'Mrs Piff, just a moment. Could we have a photograph?' I was ushered into a room, and sat on a chair. A young lady held up a bright light and the photographer asked me to remove my eyepad. A few flashes later, I replaced the pad and was on my way.

Chris bundled the suitcase and children into the car and very carefully eased me into the seat and fastened me in. He wrapped a rug around my knees and asked the children to please be quiet.

The journey home was like a nightmare. The vibrations in my head were terrible. I wanted to sleep and I couldn't rest my head. I thought the journey would never come to an end. At last Chris opened the front door and took the children in. He opened the door of the car and took me in his arms. He carried me along the path and into the house, then he went straight upstairs and laid me on our bed.

The relief at being home, at being alive and in my own bedroom was more than I could believe. I lay on my tummy, spread-eagled on the bed and cried and cried. But they were not tears of sorrow or despair. They were tears of relief and of deliverance.

Chapter Eleven

The week after my return home I had the most frightening experience I think I have ever lived through. The pain in the left side of my head and face became unbearable. I survived as a zombie, begging for more tablets so that I could sleep. I couldn't eat as I felt sick continuously.

At last I had to visit Professor Harrison in Grays Inn Road. It was pouring with rain, torrential, continuous deluges of water. The effort of getting dressed was enough, but the journey through London in those conditions was just too bad to describe. As soon as we arrived the sister on the ward put me straight to bed. Professor Harrison had been delayed at Dublin Airport and wouldn't be there until the afternoon. I went straight to sleep.

Chris and I were both given lunch and then sent downstairs to the clinic to see Professor Harrison. The Professor greeted us like old friends but, needless to say, I didn't feel much like an old friend. I told him about the pain. To my utter astonishment he said, 'No such thing as pain. There's one good thing about this operation, I practically took a blow lamp to your head and removed all the tissue. There's nothing left to give you pain.'

With that statement he removed my eyepad and proceeded to examine my eye socket. 'Skin's breaking up. That's the trouble after radiation, the skin is so fragile.'

Chris, thank the Lord, was sitting well behind me. The Professor then asked me to remove my obturator. I did and the nurse was there instantly with a receiver.

'Lean back, and for goodness sake don't move, or we will both be on the floor!'

I must admit, it was a pretty difficult thing to do, looking up into the roof of my mouth whilst I was sitting down. Professor Harrison peered with his torch and just murmured to himself.

As I replaced my obturator I mentioned to Professor Harrison that it didn't fit very well any more. He suggested I visited the dental hospital, just down the road.

'Can't I go back to Mr Issa at Wexham Park?' I asked.

'Yes of course,' he said. And that was that.

I was bitterly disappointed. I was hoping for an answer to the nagging pain in my head and had received none. How I wished I could see Mr Wallace. I was very cross and angry at being told that there was no such thing as pain. Did he think I was pretending?

The drugs succeeded in putting me to sleep, but whenever I was conscious the pain was so terrible I was aware of nothing else at all. The days were spent sitting with my head in my hands, rocking to and fro. Every day I followed the strict routine of cleaning and hosing my mouth every time I ate something. I changed my eyepad, without looking at what lay underneath it.

On the Thursday afternoon, we took the familiar route to Wexham Park Hospital to see Mr Issa. We sat in the waiting room, and I gradually began to feel weaker and weaker. I awoke to find myself sitting in the dental chair and the dental nurse giving me a drink of glucose and water.

It was marvellous to see Mr Issa again. I told him briefly about the past few weeks and the fact that after the operation the obturator didn't fit too well. Mr Issa suggested that my face would slightly alter shape and it would be better to leave it a while before Harry and John made me a new lightweight acrylic prosthesis. Meanwhile, he made a slight adjustment to the wires which fitted around my upper teeth, making the prosthesis more secure.

I told him about the nurses' enthusiasm for my prosthesis and how proud I was of it. He laughed and said that it was nice to know someone appreciated him!

It was a dull old day for our next journey to London. The pain in my head was no better and I was feeling weaker with each day that went by. Chris was very quiet, he was so patient and tolerant of me. If it hadn't been for him I would have given up the fight. He sat behind my chair in Professor Harrison's room as I told him in very definite terms that the pain in my head had not ceased since I had seen him last week and that I was not imagining it at all.

The Professor looked at me kindly and patted my hand. 'I'm sure you're not my dear.' He removed the eyepad and proceeded to swab the eyelid. Then he took a piece of gauze and put small pieces of purple-coloured tissue on to it. 'It's that radiation. The skin is so fragile it is as thin as tissue paper.'

Then I told him that I couldn't hear with my left ear.

'Now don't worry about this pain in your head. It is the exposed tissue, and if need be we can take a skin graft from your forehead and line the orbit. It will simply mean you wearing your hairstyle over your forehead.'

I sat there bewildered at this man's attitude. Was all this because of the operation? 'Oh yes, your ear, that's due to the operation. Don't worry about that, I can do a little operation to fix that.'

I couldn't believe my ears. Here I was, having lost my eye, lost my cheekbone and half my teeth and upper jaw, half my palate, deaf in one ear and rapidly going bald and this giant of a man, with the confidence of God himself, tells me not to worry, he'll fix it!

The Professor then explained that the orbit should be seen regularly, and this long journey to London was not really sensible. He suggested that I go back to Mr Wallace.

The following week, I duly turned up at Wexham Park and I sat outside with Chris, in the same area where we had sat before being told about the maxillectomy. My name was called and as I walked through the door, the first person I saw was Mr Wallace, arms outstretched as he came towards me and took my hand.

'How are you? It's so nice to see you.'

I wanted to cry out, *why won't this pain go away?* The nurse took me to a chair and I sat down. I looked up, and there was Dr Strickland, standing in front of me too. He didn't say a word. He took my head in his hands and looked at my face. 'Where is the pain?'

I told him it was all over the left side of my head. He touched it gently, and without any change of expression he walked away. Mr Wallace came to me. He took off the eyepad and examined the orbit. Not much was said. Mr Wallace explained that the eye needed to be cleaned regularly. He was unable to do it tomorrow, but he arranged for Sister Smith on Ward Eight to do it for me, and he would see me on Thursday.

I was still surviving from one dose of tablets to the next and was feeling very unhappy. The 'old me' didn't seem to be there any more. When I got home I cried in Mummy's arms and confessed how ill I felt. No matter how I tried, the pain took over completely and I didn't seem to be in control any more. Mummy cradled me in her arms. I was so frightened.

I went quickly to bed, and, I don't know why, suddenly wanted to see my left eyelid. I sat at the dressing table and removed the eyepad. What I saw in the mirror nearly stopped my heart from beating. I held my breath and stared. Where my eyelid had been was now gone. I understood what Professor Harrison said about the tissue paper skin. In its place was a hole and just black emptiness behind it.

Matthew's voice brought me to my senses.

'Mummy, can I come in?'

Quickly I replaced the pad.

'Yes, darling of course.'

I can't remember what we talked about. All I could remember was my face. It didn't belong to a living person. How could I survive with a face like that? How could I tell the children? What was going to happen to me? I had no fight left, the endless pain in my head and nausea in my stomach seemed to be in control. There was no energy left to fight. Where was Christine? She didn't exist any more. Please God, help me, I don't want to give in, but I'm so tired and weary, please don't let me die.

Chris helped me back to bed and tucked me in. He leaned over me, and kissed me.

'Are you all right? Is the pain very bad?' He had noted my

obvious silence during the evening. I hadn't wanted to cuddle the children as I usually did, afraid my eyepad would slip and horrify them. I couldn't bring myself to tell Chris.

'No, I'm fine, just very tired, don't worry, I'll be all right.'

'Call me if you want me.' He kissed me again and left me alone.

I lay in bed waiting for sleep to rescue me. It was as if I was totally on my own, unconcerned about everything and everyone. If ever there was a time to give up, it was now. It would have been so easy to escape the battle and die. Suddenly, from the sweetness of sleep a sharp voice awakened me: 'So you want to die, do you?' it asked.

The voice sounded angry and unsympathetic. 'You've given up, after everything that has been done for you.' It was me. It was old Christine speaking, as if I was standing by the side of my bed, with long blonde hair and wearing my favourite jeans, talking to the body that lay there. There was a long silence and I lay there wide awake. The room was dark, there was nobody there. 'You're not going to let cancer beat you, are you?'

A voice in my head answered. No, I won't give up for some lousy old cells that I don't want. I'll fight with every ounce of strength I have.

A feeling of immense calm overcame me. Christine, you are not going to die. This voice I heard was not my voice. It didn't come from my head, but from deep in my heart.

Chapter Twelve

When Thursday came, I found myself back in Mr Wallace's chair, looking up at his reassuring face.

'Where are my Tillywinkles?' he asked his nurse, Heather. 'Find me some, would you.'

'What are Tillywinkles?' I asked Mr Wallace.

'They are very fine scissors, and I'm going to take a small piece of tissue from your eye for a biopsy,' he replied calmly.

I wished I hadn't asked.

Heather returned with the scissors, which looked like curved nail scissors to me. She told us that they cost £50 a pair. I felt she lay great importance to this, and I was most privileged to be snipped by them! I felt Chris turn green as Mr Wallace passed the small piece of tissue carefully to Heather, and I offered a silent prayer that there might soon be a way of making the pain in my head subside.

I was very glad to get home that day. My dear friends had not deserted me and the house remained like a florist's shop, and cards still arrived every day. So many people shared in our sadness, they were so caring and thoughtful. It wasn't until much later in the day that it dawned on me why Mr Wallace had taken a biopsy. Surely they didn't think the cancer was still there, not after the extensive operation Professor Harrison had performed?

The idea played on in my mind, irritating me throughout the remainder of the day. Obviously this pain I was having had something to do with it, especially as Professor Harrison had said I shouldn't have any pain.

I was becoming more and more anxious about cuddling the

children. Claire asked what was going to happen about my eye? I couldn't give her a proper answer. It disturbed me to know that I had at some time in the very near future to confess to the children that I had lost the eye. It made me feel sick in the stomach. How could I tell them? What would their reactions be?

After lunch I went to the bathroom to clean my mouth. This process meant removing the obturator from my mouth, scrubbing it, then cleaning my teeth and finally hosing out my mouth and cheek. It wasn't until I had finished that I saw, in the mirror, water trickling down the side of my face. My eyepad was soaking wet. I took a deep breath, and realised what had happened. Another episode to add to the nightmare. I took two tablets for the pain and crawled despondently into bed.

'Hello sleepyhead, sorry to disturb you.'

It was Dr Perry's voice I heard. Slowly, I came round and gently pulled myself up. Poor Dr Perry, he should never have been so kind to me. I sat with my knees up, buried my head on them and cried and cried.

'My face should be dead, it doesn't belong to a living person. When I hose my mouth, it comes out of my eye and when I drink it runs down my nose.'

Dr Perry was wonderful. He sat on the edge of my bed, letting me pour out every anxiety that I had kept locked away to myself. I eventually finished, ending in sobs. He didn't speak to me immediately, but waited for me to calm down.

'I think your biggest worry at the moment, Christine, is not having told the children about your eye. Would you like me to tell them?'

I refused, but we had a long conversation, and Doctor Perry's professionalism was an enormous help. Afterwards I thought about what he had said, and realised it wasn't what he had said, but what I had said, that mattered. Was he right about the children knowing about my eye?

Later that day, I told Chris about Doctor Perry's visit, omitting the bit about the water and my eye. He agreed and said that it was entirely up to me and how I felt: if I wanted to tell the children, then I should. I knew that Chris couldn't do it and it was going to be worse for him than it was for me.

*

Two days later it was Saturday. Cold and damp, the smell of winter was in the air. The only exciting thing left in November after the Guy Fawkes party is that the next big event is Christmas.

I was lying in bed, thinking about what on earth Christmas was going to be like this year, when in burst the boys. Not a big, loud burst, more of an enthusiastic ball of energy burst. I was kissed and cuddled and informed of their plans for the day.

The boys were huddled beneath the blankets and Claire was curled up like a kitten by my feet. I took a deep breath, and began.

'Children, I have something to tell you.' The bedroom door opened, and Chris came and sat on the bed, his arm around Claire. 'When I went into hospital to see if Professor Harrison could do anything for my eye, he discovered another tumour had grown behind it.' I swallowed the lump in my throat.

'Well, when Professor Harrison removed the tumour from my head, he had to remove my eye as well.'

'Oh Mummy, no!' Claire burst into tears, and threw herself upon her Daddy.

Matthew's arms were flung around my neck. 'It doesn't matter, Mummy, we still love you.'

'Well, I hope they don't give you a blue one like mine, Mummy.'

I tried to laugh amongst the tears that were welling up inside me.

'What is so wonderful, children, is that my eye has not been wasted. It has been used in a transplant, so that some blind person can see.'

'That's wonderful, Mummy,' Matthew said.

'I hope they like the colour green,' Claire added. I put my arms out to her and hugged her to me.

'Don't worry, Mummy, you'll be all right.' I looked up and Chris's eyes met mine. His smile was enough to let me know they would be fine.

'Right, last down for breakfast is a nutcase.'

Chris leapt out of the room, closely followed by Matthew and Dominic.

'Claire, you're a nutcase,' I said.

'I don't care, I want to stay with you.'

'I'm fine, Claire, I'll be better now. I was anxious about telling you about my eye. I didn't want you to be upset.'

'I'm not upset Mummy. It was a shock, that's why I cried. What's going to happen. Will you have a glass eye?'

'I'm not sure. It's early days yet. But I promise as soon as they tell me, I'll let you know. Now go on down and have breakfast.' She gave me a large hug and kissed my cheek. As she opened the door she turned around with a grin on her face. 'You're last down to breakfast. Guess who's the nutcase?'

Dr Perry's theory that I would feel better when I had told the children about my eye didn't really work. True, I was relieved that as a family we all knew about the loss of my eye. However, the pain in my head and face continued relentlessly and each day seemed to be longer than the previous one. I would look at the clock in the lounge and when I looked again only five minutes would have passed.

Back to Mr Wallace again. He was sitting in his chair, adjusting his miner's lamp around his head. (Anyone who has been to an Ear, Nose and Throat specialist will know what I mean!) Heather pulled down the blinds and switched on the light. The light was reflected by the disc strapped to Mr Wallace's forehead and presumably the light illuminated my head. Chris sat in his usual chair, over to the right and behind me. I'm sure that often the visits to Mr Wallace were worse for him than they were for me.

'The biopsy results were fine,' said Mr Wallace. 'Everything seems to be in order.'

He removed the eyepad and examined my orbit—which is what Mr Wallace called the hole in my head where my eye used to be.

Then he picked up what looked like a vacuum cleaner: a machine on to which Mr Wallace fitted different-sized instruments on the end. These tools worked like vacuum cleaner attachments. He used a very fine sucker to remove granulated tissue from my head. Granulated tissue sounds like sugar, and in a way it is. As the skin heals it forms a hard crust, which is called granulation. Mr Wallace didn't want my orbit to granulate—if that's what you call it—so, these were removed. I had also developed an infection, and Mr Wallace prescribed antibiotics. It was all very painful and I tapped my feet and drummed my fingers to try and distract myself from the discomfort. Fortunately Mr Wallace was very gentle and the ordeal didn't last long.

The weeks dragged by and only the children's return from school seemed to brighten up my day. I found it too exhausting even to bath myself, so Chris would bath me in the evening, and I could go to bed immediately afterwards. One night I sat on the side of the bed and looked at my feet.

'My toenails need trimming, pass me the scissors,' I said. Chris passed me the scissors and I bent over. But I felt suddenly dizzy and lay back on the bed. 'I'm too exhausted even to cut my own toenails.' Chris laughed and took the scissors from me.

'Feet up, come on.'

I can't remember anyone cutting my toenails before, and I can assure you it was the funniest thing ever. It tickles, for a start, and it's very hard to keep still. It took Chris ages and we giggled and chuckled for the first time in weeks.

But such moments of laughter were rare. I still felt no better. My stomach felt as if there was a thunderstorm going on inside it, and neither the thunder nor the lightning could find a way to escape.

One morning I awoke feeling absolutely ghastly. I didn't know what to do. My head hurt and my stomach was in turmoil. Chris brought me a cup of tea, but before the drink was finished, I moved faster than I had for months.

I was violently sick. It was as if my stomach had taken just enough and it contracted, expelling its entire contents. I scrubbed my mouth and hosed it as I never had before. I couldn't remember when I was last sick. It must have been when I was expecting Dominic. Well, it was not like this. My poor tummy had had enough abuse with the drugs I had been feeding it, and now finally let me know in no uncertain terms.

I crawled back to the bedroom.

'Are you all right?' Chris asked anxiously.

'Yes, I think so.' I looked at the bottle of tablets I had been given. There were two hundred of them left. 'I'm not taking one more tablet,' I told Chris. 'It's *those* horrid things that make me feel so ill and sick. I'll manage without them.'

I sipped some water and lay on the bed. I was cold, and even though my tummy felt better my head was pulsating with pain. I was soaked in perspiration and I could still smell the foul stink of vomit. I shuddered and climbed out of bed. 'I must change my eyepad,' I said, weakly.

Chris left the room: I had decided when I first saw my eye that nobody would ever see my face except Mr Wallace and Dr Perry. I loved Chris too much to let him suffer the agony of knowing the price I had to pay to survive.

I removed the pad, only to discover it soaked in vomit. I felt utter disgust. I wanted to scream. I swabbed my face and replaced the eyepad. I called out to Chris.

'Will you phone Mr Wallace's secretary and get me an appointment as fast as you can.'

'Why, what's the matter?'

'Because I've thrown up all over my head!' I couldn't be more specific, but Chris got the message and phoned immediately. We were on our way within the hour.

On our way out of the hospital, we met the social worker. She was a very sweet lady and enquired how I was. Sadly she told me that Mark, the boy I went to Mount Vernon with, was back in hospital. His cancer was terminal and there was nothing they could do, except give him pain-killing drugs. She explained that he was totally withdrawn and wouldn't speak to anyone, and asked if perhaps I would have a word with him.

'Of course I will,' I said. Taking Chris's arm we walked the long corridors. Chris said, 'Now are you sure you want to see him. It won't upset you?'

'No, I would like to see him.'

I don't know what I expected, but as I looked into Mark's eyes I found it hard to believe he was the same young boy I had met just eight months ago. He was sitting in a wheelchair, gazing ahead.

'Hallo Mark, do you remember me? Don't tell me you're still supporting Chelsea?'

The word Chelsea registered, and he looked up.

'Hello, what are you doing here?'

'I came to visit Mr Wallace for some treatment at the clinic. The social worker told me you were here, so I thought I would come and say hello. How are you?'

'Just waiting. It's all over me. They can't do anything, I'm just waiting.'

'You look so well, Mark. Your hair has grown much better than mine has. Don't just sit and wait Mark. You can fight it if you try.'

I took his hands, with their beautifully white, neatly trimmed fingernails. They were cold.

'Please try, Mark. I'll come and see you next week.'

'I won't be here.'

I kissed his cheek, and his blue eyes stared at me. 'Thank you for coming,' he said.

Oh, that poor boy, just eighteen years old. He was so resigned to dying; such a wasted life.

It was Dominic's eighth birthday that weekend. He chose to go to the National History Museum—again. Chris begged me to stay at home. I naturally told him I would be fine. I knew the Natural History Museum like the back of my hand—well nearly. There were seats everywhere. I could sit down whilst they viewed.

Saturday morning arrived, and Dominic opened his presents and cards. Mummy phoned and sang 'Happy Birthday' down the telephone. She phones us all on our birthdays—even though she sounds like an out-of-tune Gracie Fields!

Chris gave me strict instructions to stay in bed until mid-morning, before he left with Claire to do the shopping. Suddenly the phone rang and Matthew answered it. He came running upstairs.

'It's a lady for you, Mummy.' It was the social worker from Wexham Park.

'I'm sorry to disturb you Mrs Piff, but I thought you would like to know that Mark passed away this morning.'

There was a long pause. 'Thank you for letting me know.'

'He was happy at seeing you, Mrs Piff. You were very kind to him during his illness.'

I couldn't cry. I couldn't find words to describe how I felt, just very empty inside. Mark was just ten years old when I had Dominic. How unfair life was. Mark had visited Lourdes during the summer, and I hoped his faith had been some help to him at the end. I would never forget him. Every birthday Dominic had, I would remember him.

Chapter Thirteen

Christmas day was wonderful. Chris cooked the turkey beautifully, with delicious roast potatoes and parsnips. The Christmas pudding was one I had made the year before, so we called it a pre-cancer pud. The children were overwhelmed by their gifts, having thought Christmas wouldn't be so good this year with a poorly mummy. I told them that Father Christmas was never ill, and he made sure that this Christmas all their wishes would come true, as they had been so good. Not so Chris—he had three can openers!

It was hard to believe that a whole year had passed, and here we were celebrating once more. For Chris and me it was a very special celebration. The past year had been filled with nightmares that one could never have believed possible. We had survived one tragedy after another and come out smiling.

My parents had chosen to spend Christmas on their own, so for the very first time in our married life we were just the five of us. There seemed to be a much closer bond between us all. Every moment was shared and treasured. I wanted the day to last forever.

Once Christmas was over, I set my heart on going to the New Year's Ball at Wellington College again. We had had such a wonderful time the year before. I knew that all my friends would be there, and it was thanks to them that I was able to share in the festivities again. I desperately wanted to show them how well I was, and how determined I was to get back to my normal life again.

I asked Mr Wallace if I could go, and he said, 'Go late and leave early.'

Determined to go I spent the afternoon in bed. I wore the same dress as the year before, although Mummy insisted that this time I wore a vest! I would do anything so long as they let me go.

It was cold and frosty and I wrapped my shawl around me as I walked into the large hall. It was super to see everyone, all the familiar faces. I had threatened to put sequins on my eyepad to add glamour to the occasion: I was so aware of it and felt I stuck out like a sore thumb. But when friends came over to our table and sat and chatted to us, I felt so welcome. I watched them dancing and remembered last year.

'May I have this dance?' Ray took my hand.

'I don't think I can dance, Ray.'

'Don't worry.'

The music they played was soft and slow. Ray took me in his arms and we just went round and round, hardly lifting our feet from the floor. People were throwing streamers and the room was littered with brightly-coloured garlands.

Ray said, 'Enough?' I nodded my head and we started to walk back to the table. We couldn't. We both looked down to see what was the matter. Our feet had wound around yards and yards of streamers, like forks with spaghetti wound around them. We roared with laughter as we untangled ourselves from the paper.

Thus we saw 1978 in. I fought back the tears, and everyone kissed everyone else. Three balloons for the children. It was time to go home and Chris steered me through the dancers. Just as we reached the door, Pam, the secretary at the Infant School, took my arm. She kissed us both and wished us a happy New Year, and said, 'Let it be a hundred times better than 1977.'

'I don't know Pam, '77 wasn't so bad,' I said. 'It has made me realise how lucky I am.' And I knew as I said it that I really meant it.

The infection in my orbit was persistent, to say the least. Even the antibiotics were of no use in clearing it. Then, at my next session with Mr Wallace, he produced a magic spray.

'This will help to get rid of the infection,' he said, as he shook the aerosol can. I lacked confidence. It was bad enough having the orbit cleaned, let alone have an aerosol sprayed into it. Oh, well, grit your teeth and here we go.

The sensation I felt is indescribable.

'If I fall on the floor with my legs and arms in the air twitching like mad, you'll know I'm done for.'

This ordeal went on for weeks.

Gradually the pain in my head turned more to discomfort rather than pain and I wasn't taking any tablets at all. My appetite was back to normal, although I couldn't bear the smell or taste of coffee. I grew completely intolerant of cigarettes and nobody was allowed to smoke in our home. My life-saver was hot chocolate. I drank two pints of milk a day and always with chocolate.

I celebrated my birthday in January and the children gave me their individual presents. Dominic's was a pencil with a rubber lead. Matthew gave me plastic matches that didn't strike and Claire gave me sugar cubes that floated in my tea. The children tried these out on everyone who came to the house. Mummy and Daddy gave me a fur coat. I couldn't believe it. It wasn't real fur, but a beautiful imitation. I asked Chris if I could wear a fur coat with blue jeans. He gave me a disapproving look. I must admit when I first put the coat on I felt like Popeye's Olive Oyl.

Mr Issa said that it was time to fit a new prosthesis for my mouth, so appointments were made and the great day came. I was rather nervous at breakfast with the children.

Dominic with his usual logic said, 'I don't know what you're worried about, Mummy. It could be much worse. You could have to wear a brace.'

I agreed, and promised to be good and said if we were home in time, we would meet them from school.

At Wexham Park Mr Issa was eager to begin. Jean, his assistant, mixed up the pink powder and gave it to him.

'We have to move fast, as this is a quick setting paste.'

How you take a cast of an upper jaw when there isn't one there, I don't know. It was soon over, and I commented on how wonderful that powder would be for an obstinate soufflé. Harry and John, the technicians, came in and we chatted and joked. Harry asked, 'How's the hole in your head?'

'Do you mind. Let's call it orbit now, please,' I retorted.

Chris and I washed the dishes together after supper that night, all five of us in the kitchen. I was washing up and we were all chatting. Chris opened the cupboard to my left and replaced dried dishes into it. Not aware of this, as I couldn't see, I turned my head to the left and banged it on the cupboard door. It did hurt! I was so mad, not because it hurt, but because I had been so stupid, that I picked up a saucepan off the cooker and opened the back door. I hurled that saucepan as far as I could down the garden. The children stood there not saying a word, mouths open, speechless.

Chris walked out, picked up the saucepan and came back into the kitchen. 'Feel better now?' And, of course, I did.

Now begin all the frustrations of adjusting to one eye. With just one eye you lose the three-dimensional effect. Everything is flat. I would pour milk into a glass and carry on until it overflowed. Even placing a cup on to a table was a hazard. I had to train myself into thinking about everything I did. I would become so angry with myself whenever I did something stupid.

Chris supervised all the cooking. To remove anything from the oven was dangerous. To be treated like an idiot didn't help. I was so frustrated. I couldn't judge correctly how to hook my coat hangers over the rail in my wardrobe. My arms would ache. Inevitably I would give in, throwing the clothes on the floor, kicking the wardrobe, then collapsing in tears. In time I learned to pick myself up, dust myself down, and start all over again.

Matthew's birthday came round again—his eleventh. The War Museum was his choice this year. Claire and I were not too enthusiastic, though we tried hard not to show it. I suggested that perhaps we could go into a McDonalds and have a hamburger afterwards, which succeeded in cheering us up. I filled up a thermos with hot chocolate and made cold drinks for the children.

The five of us set off on our journey, a busman's holiday for poor Chris—having to drive to London at the weekend is a real sacrifice. I was impressed with the outer building of the museum. But while the boys were fascinated by the displays Claire and I just wandered from room to room.

Afterwards we went to the nearest McDonalds and ate huge hamburgers. Matthew said that I couldn't possibly have a milk shake there, as they were so thick that I wouldn't be able to suck hard enough!

'I'll show you,' I retorted. 'I'll have a large chocolate milk shake, please.'

But he was right, of course, and the three of them carried my milk shake off to share on the way home.

That evening, Chris and I sat quietly together after the children had gone to bed. I was exhausted. It had been a very tiring day and I was finding it more and more difficult to cope with people staring at me. I wanted to run away and hide, but I knew this was not the answer. The more I went out and mixed with people the better. But the anxiety seemed to drain me of what small amount of energy I had, and I was finding it more and more difficult to cope.

Was it really a year since we had trudged around Avebury Downs, I wondered. So much had happened since then, and it was hard to imagine that we had survived so much. I was grateful we couldn't see into the future. If Mr Wallace had told me then what was going to happen to me, I don't know what I would have done. Probably simply not believed him. Yet, as I thought about it, I realised that everyone has their problems in life, and they have to cope with them. Who knows—even Mr Wallace himself.

These episodes left me totally drained of energy, and the only remedy was to sleep. I was fed up with that damned eyepad. I dreamed at night about losing it and horrifying people. I would awaken to find I had torn it off, and would be sitting up crying. Thank God Chris slept soundly through those times.

Chris took us out for drives on Sundays, and we would walk in woods and around lakes. I never would have believed how difficult it could be to walk over grass that looks beautifully smooth and even. The children laughed when I fell over or tripped up, it was quite infuriating. The only consolation was that I was permitted to sit down and recover whilst they charged around like puppies off their leads.

Mr Wallace was delighted with my progress, so I didn't bother him with the emotional side and the problems I was having. However, I did tell him that the eyepad was only just covering the orbit now and I felt most insecure when I was outside.

He gave the problem some thought and suggested I go to the hospital where they specialised in eyes. I was advised to report there the following Tuesday.

As we walked into the entrance hall, there were two nurses at the desk, and one male nurse who looked up as I entered and pointed down the corridor. 'Eye clinic down there,' he said.

'I don't want to go to the eye clinic. I wish to speak to the sister in charge.' One of the nurses at the desk asked me what I wanted. Chris told them of Mr Wallace, and said that I was to speak to the sister who knew all about it. It was like looking at a blank wall.

'I don't know anything about that,' said the nurse, and she carried on sorting through files.

Chris asked the other nurse if we could speak to the sister in charge. The nurse called to a woman dressed in dark blue who had just arrived on the scene. 'What's the matter?' she asked. Chris patiently repeated the message, explaining that Mr Wallace had told us to come here and that the sister was going to be able to advise us on our problem over wearing the eyepad.

The nurse looked at me and said coldly, 'Wear dark glasses.'

'If I wear glasses they assist in pushing the eye pad into the orbit,' I replied.

'Take the eye pad off then.'

'But I have lost my eye.'

'It doesn't matter. Nobody can see.'

Before I leapt at the woman and punched her on the nose, I stormed out of the hospital with Chris in hot pursuit. I sat in the car infuriated and ready to explode with a rage the world had not yet seen. I looked at Chris, and burst into tears. I cried and cried. Oh God, did nobody understand?

On the following visit to Mr Wallace, he produced two eye shields with black elastic carefully and neatly attached to them, which he suggested I try over the eyepad.

'It certainly will help if I go out in the rain,' I said. I wanted to giggle when I looked in the mirror—I did look funny.

The children thought I looked hilarious. I tucked one leg up and did a pathetic imitation of Jim lad, pretending to speak to the parrot on my shoulder. The boys took turns in trying out my shields, and thought they were nearly as much fun as when I had the monocle.

By this time my hair was pretty revolting. Claire was heartbroken when she combed it for me and discovered the large bald patch underneath my long, thin locks. I explained to her how radiation destroyed not only the cancer cells, but also living cells like hair. Fortunately the hair would grow again.

Nearly every evening Claire would lift up my hair to see if it was growing. One very exciting moment came when, on her usual investigative trip, Claire discovered a layer of fluff on my head. Gradually, the hair was coming through.

'Oh it's beautiful, Mummy. It's golden brown and it's curly,' Claire exclaimed.

We all laughed at the prospect of me with a patch of curls while the remainder of my hair stayed straight. But I decided then to have my hair trimmed and as I didn't feel confident enough to go to a hairdresser, I phoned a friend and asked if the man who cut her hair would come and cut mine at home.

When he arrived I explained my predicament to him and he combed my hair through.

'I won't cut it short then. I'll just trim it until the new hair is a bit longer,' he said.

Six weeks later, out came the scissors again, and all my hair was snipped off. I couldn't remember when I had last worn my hair short. It must have been ten years, when Matthew was tiny. As Ian dried my hair, a little miracle happened. My hair went curly. It was unbelievable. Claire was bubbling with excitement, 'Mummy, Mummy, its lovely!'

I looked in the mirror and was unrecognisable. The difference in having my hair cut was remarkable. Ian told me it was the best thing to have done, to cut it really short.

I thanked him profusely, because suddenly I began to feel like a woman again. I looked at Claire, and took her hands in mine.

'See Claire. Cancer gives you curls.'

Chapter Fourteen

It was early September and the end of the summer holidays. I felt particularly sad that year that the children were going back to school. Then the phone rang, and it was my great friend, Dorothy.

'How do you fancy a walk and a picnic? I could pick you up around twelve.'

I thought it was a lovely idea, especially as I knew it would take my mind off the empty house. Chris thought we were mad, and didn't hesitate to tell me so, but I was delighted to see Dot. I checked I had my front door key—it would never do to be locked out on my first day—and we set off.

'Thought we'd take a walk along the canal. I know a pretty walk we can go on,' Dot said as she parked the car in a churchyard, and slung a haversack across her shoulders.

We set off, climbing over stiles and narrow footpaths rarely used: it was just like being a Brownie again. Eventually we came to a huge field, surrounded on all sides by magnificent trees. Two-thirds of the way across the field Dot stopped.

'This looks as good a place as any.' She dropped the rucksack on the long grass and sat down. Inside were two plastic ground sheets. They were jolly comfortable. We sat in silence listening to the birds. It was so peaceful—such a sane thing to do. I wished there was a rule that every overtired, worn-out mother should take herself off on a picnic when the little 'dears' return to school. It is so much more peaceful without them. Dorothy produced a little stove with a kettle and brewed real tea—none of your thermos flasks for us. We had rolls and cheese, tomatoes and fruit. The tea tasted wonderful. We sat there, giggling at what fun we were having whilst all the other mums were back at work. Even when it began to rain on us we continued our lunch, undaunted. In fact, it was even more fun.

After lunch we packed up our debris and walked along the canal bank. The rain made patterns on the water, and the verges were weighed down with the heavy grasses of summer. It was an exciting place, and I invented the most exciting stories in my mind. It was just like being a child again. At last rain stopped play, and it was time to go home. The stiles felt like church spires to climb and I lost my balance a few times. Nevertheless it was a lovely day and I was so grateful to Dorothy for the wonderful idea. It is an afternoon I will treasure forever.

The children were amazed we had been out without them: it was rather like playing truant.

I had been getting 'away pains'—as Mr Wallace called them—for a long time. It was a very strange sensation: I couldn't feel the left side of my head or forehead at all. Mr Wallace explained that nerves were funny things and once they were damaged it took a long time for them to heal. My upper lip on the left side was still numb, and so was what was left of the cheek above it. My nose still continued to run, and my hanky was my best friend and went with me everywhere. I asked Mr Wallace about the whistling sounds I had in my ear. When I put my head on the pillow, it sounded like feet marching up and down. I had always had sounds in my left ear, but since I had had an ear infection earlier in the year it hadn't really stopped.

'Oh yes, there's a name for noises in the ear,' he said. 'It has been known to drive people mad.'

I sat there looking at Mr Wallace, and I wanted to laugh. It was rather like a mechanic telling you your engine is loose, but not to worry, if it fell out you might crash, although then again you might not. Mr Wallace seemed to think my engine would stay intact—I wasn't so sure.

Then he said, 'Well Christine, I think it's time to start thinking about your prosthesis.' My heart started beating so fast I thought it would deafen us all. 'The orbit is epithelialising—

that's making new skin—beautifully and I think Harry could make you a temporary prosthesis to be going on with.'

I nearly ran down the corridor to the laboratory to see Harry and John and excitedly told them what Mr Wallace had said. Harry said it wasn't possible to make a temporary prosthesis, it would have to be the real thing. Then he asked me to remove my eyepad. I really didn't want to, but he showed no reaction whatsoever, and neither did John. I silently thanked them for that. After they had examined me I replaced the eyepad and asked what they proposed doing.

Harry confidently told me how they would make an acrylic base which would fit inside the orbit and another outer frame which would hold the eye. It all sounded too much for me.

'I'll have a word with Mr Wallace and then we'll fix an appointment for you to come. Any day, any time, whenever it suits you, Chris. For you, nothing's too much trouble.'

Dear Harry, if only he knew how frightened I was! I thought and thought about it for a week until I saw Mr Wallace again.

I explained how tender the orbit still was and that I didn't feel ready for Harry to make the prosthesis. When I had seen Professor Harrison he had said that the opticians, Clement Clarke, could make a prosthesis which incorporated glasses. This is what I really wanted.

Bless Mr Wallace; he said he would sort it out. The thought of anyone other than Mr Wallace made me feel very nervous. Once during the year he hadn't been able to clean the orbit for me. Another doctor had taken over, and I had been a nervous gibbering idiot by the time they had finished. After that I decided to clean the orbit myself.

I bought some cotton buds and applied the cream we had now progressed to, having abandoned the super fly spray. It was an ordeal at first, but gradually it became just another routine, like cleaning my mouth. Because of this, I was aware of the discomfort I would have to endure whilst a prosthesis was being made.

Mr Wallace asked if I would be available to visit Clement Clarke. I nearly leapt out of the chair with enthusiasm and bombarded Mr Wallace with questions, none of which he could answer. At last, to be able to discard the eyepad, it was too good to be true! The children would be so pleased; I couldn't wait to tell them.

We arrived at Clement Clarke's the following week, and were ushered upstairs. The lift door opened on to a small landing, on which was a small desk with a typewriter on it, and lots of papers and notes. An elderly, white-haired man, dressed in a white coat stood waiting for us. He wore very old-fashioned spectacles, which sat on the end of his nose.

We walked into a tiny square room with a chair in the centre. This faced a large window and the sill served as a surface for mirror, lamp and tissues. On the wall behind the chair was a glass frame full of photographs of people's heads. Chris looked at them, I wished I hadn't.

Chris left me sitting on the chair and promised to return at midday: I had been told I would be required to stay all day. The butterflies in my tummy wouldn't settle, though I tried to remain calm and detached. Mr Young, the technician, had to make a mould of my cheek and orbit up to my eyebrow. As he put a plastic bib around my neck, he warned me that I wouldn't much like the next bit. The eyepad was removed and replaced with what looked like a handful of mud! Then all the edges by my nose and brow were smoothed out—it seemed as if he was sculpting a face. It felt wet and cold, but that was the only discomfort. Then Mr Young went to fill in the mould with wax. All the materials he used set very quickly, rather like that which Mr Issa had used for my obturator.

For the next step out came a little square box, inside which were all the coloured eyes one could imagine. Except mine. Mr Young gazed into my eye.

'Hmm, it's green and grey, most unusual.'

'Don't give me a blue one, I promised Dominic I wouldn't have a blue one,' I murmured to myself. I hadn't realised that not only are eyes a different colour, but also a different shape. Mr Young had to find an eye the correct shape, and a proper colour match. He painstakingly painted the eye to match my own in every detail.

Then the mould was placed into my orbit and Mr Young set to work. With a very fine tool he cut away into the wax reproducing my eye and cheekbones. Into the eye socket was fitted the eye, which was the most difficult thing to do. He seemed to spend hours replacing, adjusting and trying to get the eye in the right position to match my own.

Mr Young didn't stop for lunch, he worked without a break until 4.30, when we went downstairs to choose some suitable spectacles. I knew exactly what I wanted so it took less than ten minutes to make up my mind.

I had never felt so shattered. I had sat in the chair for six hours, with only two cups of tea and a bar of chocolate. Chris took me home to three disappointed children.

I didn't realise at the time what psychological pressure these visits to Clement Clarke put on me. I became very bad-tempered and had violent outbursts if things went wrong. I was making up at the dressing table one evening when Chris called to see if I was ready. I was so angry at being disturbed, I threw my lipstick at the mirror. Fortunately, it missed the mirror, but it smashed the fluorescent light which was underneath the glass and it splintered into pieces.

I burst into tears. I couldn't understand my behaviour and was thoroughly ashamed of my uncontrollable temper. I was so unhappy and not in the least bit excited at the prospect of my new glasses.

The children enquired constantly about my new eye and glasses. I told them of the process, and how the glasses would cover the prosthesis.

'Will it blink?' asked Dominic.

'Only when she tips forward, and says "Mama",' Chris said, trying to make light of the conversation.

'You'll look like Wonder Woman, Mummy, with big glasses.'

'No, I think I'll be more like Bionic Woman, Matthew. I'll be able to focus my eye in your direction and see what you're doing in the playground.'

'Like my Action Man, Mummy. You can look through the back of his head and see out of his eye.'

'Well, I don't think I'll be able to do that, darling. I do have something in my head, despite what Daddy says.'

The children were really looking forward to seeing this face of mine with two eyes. They were as irritated by the eyepad as I was, and were equally angry when people stared at me. The sooner I had my prosthesis, the better.

On my return to Mr Young I saw my glasses on the windowsill, and a flutter of excitement bubbled up from my tummy.

'Will it be ready today?'

'Yes, if we get started,' he said.

'Have you made lots of eye prostheses?' I asked.

'Oh, yes, I've been at it for a long time. Since the war, in fact. I'm retiring in March and they are not going to replace me. They are closing the department down because they can't find anyone to replace me. Nobody wants to know nowadays.'

Mr Young showed me an ear that he had made for a patient, and told me of the noses he made. I couldn't believe it. So many unfortunate people that, thanks to this man's skill, were made whole again. What a loss he would be.

Again it took all day, fitting and making adjustments. The most difficult part was putting the glasses on over the prosthesis and glueing them together. I thought my back would break as he pushed the bridge of the glasses hard against the prosthesis waiting for it to set. It had to be un-stuck and redone four times.

I hadn't seen the prosthesis closely before and I knew it wouldn't be long before I could look into the mirror and see my face with two eyes. Chris came into the room and sat behind me. Mr Young said he could have a look.

I looked up into Chris's face and he smiled. Too late, I had seen the disappointment on his face. Then Mr Young told me to look in the mirror. Deep breath. The eye was good, but it looked too small. I didn't feel happy, yet how could I criticise Mr Young's work?

The eye looked small to me and more closed than my real eye. 'Have they put the same lenses in the glasses as in my right eye?' I asked, reluctantly.

'Let's go downstairs and see the manager. Perhaps a slight adjustment to the glasses will help.'

But the manager said that the lenses were both the same.

'In that case, the eye is too small and too closed,' I said.

'Yes you're right,' the receptionist, who had come too, agreed. 'I'll tell him, don't worry. He's very tired, and I keep telling him to have his eyes tested.'

Despite my bitter disappointment I stifled a giggle. Here we were in one of the biggest and best opticians in London, and poor Mr Young needed his eyes testing.

Another appointment was made for November. Poor Mr Young had to scrap the first prosthesis and start all over again. But by 5.30 that afternoon I was wearing my glasses and my new eye. It was incredible. This time the results were a resounding success and we were all delighted. I promised faithfully to wear it all the time. Never, ever again would I wear my eyepad except in bed.

It was dark on the journey home. I was so excited to have my eye at last. But mixed up with all the excitement was a lot of apprehension. I had to walk indoors and see the children. What would they think? Would they like it?

At last we were home. Chris opened the front door. Great activity from the lounge, but I flew straight upstairs, catching a view of Matthew's face as I rushed by.

'She's got them, she's got them,' he cried.

Chris called him back from following me. I looked at myself in the mirror for a long time. Please God, may they like it, I thought. Then I took a deep breath and walked into the lounge. The three of them stood side by side, staring, mouths open.

'Well. What do you think?'

'Mummy, your glasses are super,' exclaimed Claire.

Matthew said, 'It looks so real!'

Dominic—no comment.

I collapsed on the couch, and they surrounded me like a swarm of bees.

'Does it blink?' 'Are you looking at me?' 'What happens when you close your eyes?' 'You look cross-eyed.' 'I love the colour, Mummy. It looks just like your real eye.'

'Has it got eyelashes? Are they painted on?' 'Where's your eyebrow?' 'It looks funny from here. I can see the join.' 'What does it feel like?'

I was bombarded with these questions and comments. I had no time for answers. Chris just sat there, with a wry grin on his face.

Eventually I was allowed to escape into the kitchen to prepare supper. When I saw my reflection in the kitchen window, it looked a very unfamiliar but very welcome sight.

As we sat and ate that evening there was a continuous conversation about my glasses.

Matthew said, 'John's coming round tomorrow to do his science homework, and look at your eye. I told the boys at school. Can they all come and have a look too?'

'I told the girls, Mum. I couldn't concentrate at school, I thought about you all day. I can't wait for you to go up to school. I'll tell all the teachers you have it at last.'

Dominic's turn. 'I think I'll tell Ian first, or James. Are you looking at me, Mummy?'

The remainder of the evening was spent with the children sitting staring at my face. Criticising, praising and being painfully honest.

'Please would you put some make-up on it, Mummy?'

'Can I have a look at it when you take it off, Mummy?' That was Matthew.

'It doesn't have any wrinkles like your real one.' Trust Dominic.

My orbit suddenly irritated, and I experienced the awful sensation of needing to scratch, but having nothing to scratch— very frustrating. I touched my prosthesis and felt my eyelashes. It was exciting, I even pretended to have an eyelash in my eye, and acted out a stupid scene. The children laughed, they were so happy for me.

I took them up to bed. Dominic was in bed and Matthew was sitting by his feet. 'When you look down at Matthew, Mummy, your new eye is still looking at me.'

I kissed them good night and went downstairs. I sat down next to Chris.

'Well, darling, that's over. After those comments and criticisms I think I can face the world.'

In the privacy of my own room, I had the first opportunity to examine the prosthesis carefully. The hours of work Mr Young had spent on painting the eye were well rewarded: it was exactly the same as my own eye, the colour and all the detail was there. Only one complaint, the eyelashes were not as long as my own! It was rather tricky making the eye up with my cosmetics so I decided to play safe and not use the golden yellow shadow I had been using. I chose a powdered green, a dull shade that could easily be applied with a cotton bud.

There was no way I could disguise the prosthesis, the colour was not my skin colour and I would have to grow my hair longer and sweep it towards my face.

Claire approved the make-up and I prepared myself for the outside world. Our first visit was to take Matthew to a football match at school. It was early on a Saturday morning. Thick fog enveloped all of Crowthorne and not a soul was about.

'This is ridiculous Matthew, you can't possibly play football in this fog.'

'It will clear, Mum, and talking about ridiculous, I bet you are the only person in Crowthorne wearing sun glasses!'

Cheeky monkey, he was just out of reach as my arm flew past him! We dropped him off with the remainder of his team and returned home.

'Well, that wasn't too bad was it?'

'Not at all. I guess God fixed the weather for me this morning, so I could still hide.'

It really is so difficult to explain how I felt, facing everyone. I had been waiting for the opportunity to have my new prosthesis and to abandon the dreaded eyepad for so long, and now here I was, more anxious than ever. The fact was, I suppose, I had hidden behind that eyepad. People knew I had lost my eye, but didn't realise just how much of my face was missing. Only Mr Wallace, Doctor Perry and I really knew. Now, I had to go out and face the world, exposing myself and revealing the truth.

It was all totally unnecessary. Friends and neighbours who

came to see me didn't comment. A few of them said how they liked my glasses and one sat and examined me thoroughly, making me feel like some monster out of a horror movie. I wanted and needed everyone to tell me how fabulous it was, and when they ignored it I felt cross. On the other hand if they did mention it I became a nervous wreck. It was a very difficult time. There was no pleasing me. Only the children made me laugh. I had hoped by some magic I wouldn't be so stupid when doing things, like walking into cupboard doors, pouring wine on to the table and missing the glass; or pouring sugar into the container and not stopping in time before it poured over the top. I couldn't thread needles to save my life and on mentioning the frustration of this to Mr Wallace, he said, 'Really, I thought you closed one eye when you threaded a needle!' No sympathy from him.

When I next went to Wexham Park Heather was so excited she didn't know what to do.

'It's marvellous, it's wonderful!' Chris looked anxious and he didn't let me out of his sight. I smiled at him and shrugged my shoulders. Dear Heather, she had waited for my glasses as long as I had. She just didn't realise the trauma I was going through.

Mr Wallace walked down the corridor, but whereas he usually smiled in recognition when he saw me, today he strode quickly into his room.

'He probably didn't recognise you with your glasses on,' said Chris and buried his head back into his magazine. If the truth was told, Chris was as excited as I was at showing Mr Wallace the glasses, but he wouldn't say so.

Heather, still bubbling called, 'Come in, Christine.' I walked in, followed by Chris. Mr Wallace looked up, pushed back his chair, crossed over his legs and smiled.

'Very good, mmm, *very* good.' And that was it. Nothing else—men!

After my appointment with Mr Wallace I went to show off my new face to Harry and John. They were greatly impressed and asked how Mr Young had fitted the prosthesis to the glasses. 'It's very good,' said Harry. 'The eye is perfect,' commented John. I could have kissed them. Praise at last from two people I held in great esteem. Harry, John, Mr Young and all technicians like them are artists in their work. Their skill and pride in producing a prosthesis as life-like as possible is remarkable.

I can never thank them enough.

Chapter Fifteen

One Sunday night Dominic came downstairs and asked if I would go up and talk to Matthew.

'Now what's the matter?' I asked as I followed Dominic into the bedroom. Sure enough, Matthew was sobbing away, unable to tell me what was the matter. Claire joined us and acted as a social worker, trying to analyse all his worries. We didn't come to a solution, so I kissed him good night and left Claire and Dominic talking to him.

More tears in the morning. Oh Lord, this is all I need. I couldn't get through to Matthew and find out what was troubling him. He clung to me sobbing. I couldn't get him out of the front door, he clung to me, begging not to be sent to school. I did, of course, only to find him on the doorstep half an hour later.

This went on for a week. I phoned the school and spoke to Mrs Walker, the Head of Year. She explained that Matthew had not been very happy on the school trip, but nothing had happened to cause a reaction like this. She suggested that we might have a chat with the school psychiatrist.

Matthew grew progressively worse. He ran away from school twice, although he couldn't explain why he was so unhappy. During the evenings he sat quietly in the chair with me until bedtime. He cried himself to sleep every night. Dominic and Claire were really so kind and understanding. How they carried on their lives so happily I will never know.

Chris took Matthew to school every day and Matthew was delivered to Mrs Walker's office. He spent his day with her, doing school work and helping her. She was an angel of mercy—I don't know how we could have coped with the situation if it hadn't been for her patience and understanding.

I gave up trying to analyse Matthew, I was far too close to him for that. Chris and I decided we would give him another week and if there was no improvement we would take him to see Dr Perry, who understood us as a family better than any psychiatrist could.

The next evening, supper was very quiet. Chris was anxious about his work and I was concerned about Matthew's sudden outburst of unhappiness. The children didn't speak, except the boys to complain about the spaghetti. Dominic in particular hated it, and all around his plate were bits of food. As I looked at the pile of left-over spaghetti waiting in the kitchen to be cleared away, I felt like exploding. The children, guessing my mood, disappeared upstairs. I looked at the ghastly mess. I would have loved to have thrown it out of the back door, but it was too revolting to consider, especially as I would have had to clean it up!

'Claire, Matthew, Dominic, come here at once!' I called out.

Their feet thundered down the stairs and they stood straight-faced in front of me.

'Claire, fetch the blue handbag that Grandma gave to me.'

Claire returned with the handbag.

'Here, Matthew, hold it.'

I opened the bag and scraped all the left-over spaghetti inside. The children's faces were priceless. I snapped the bag shut and took it out to the dustbin and dropped it in.

As I walked back into the kitchen, the children were still open-mouthed.

'That will be a surprise for the dustman,' Claire said, and started to giggle.

'Mummy, you're mad,' said Matthew.

'What's Grandma going to say when you tell her?'

'I'm not going to tell her. It was a silly bag anyway. It was so narrow you couldn't even put a purse into it. It was just made for spaghetti.'

We all laughed together, and a lot of the earlier tension was over. Dominic couldn't wait to tell Chris.

Chris's reply to him was, 'Nothing your mother does could surprise me.'

Matthew's problems were not over, he seemed to be getting worse. It was heartbreaking to see him like this. Chris was wonderful with him. He was calm and determined and left no doubt in Matthew's mind that he was going to school, come what may.

One particular morning Matthew was really angry. He didn't want to go to school, he wasn't going to leave me. I was at my wits' end, my emotions torn to shreds.

Matthew looked at me and said, 'If you send me to school, I'll run away again.'

My right hand slapped his face so hard, he wondered what had hit him. I felt sick. I can't remember when I last hit him, I disapprove of physical violence and have never found it necessary to hit the children. Immediately I apologised and he went quietly to school.

An hour later there was a phone call. Where was Matthew? Chris drove around the village, but couldn't find him. The phone rang again. It was Mrs Walker.

'Matthew said he would hide in the woods at the bottom of the garden,' she told us. And sure enough, when Chris went, there was Matthew. He was like a tiny, crumpled animal as he walked up through the garden bent and dejected. His eyes met mine, and they were filled with fear and anguish.

I longed to throw my arms around him and keep him with me for ever, but I knew this wasn't the answer. I thought my heart would burst, the pain was so great.

I made him a drink, and Chris told him to wash his hands and face, because he was going back to school. Matthew knew better than to question his father, and went meekly back to his classroom.

When he had gone I phoned and made an appointment to see Dr Perry. He was very kind, and agreed to see us as soon as possible. When we arrived at his surgery, Dr Perry told Chris and me to leave the room, he wished to speak to Matthew alone.

Twenty minutes later Matthew came for us and said Dr Perry wished to see us.

'Consider what has happened to him during the last year,' he told us. 'The thought his mother may die. It's not surprising he is showing some reaction. I have reassured him that you're not about to die and I hope he believes me. Come and see me again whenever you need to.'

Poor sensitive Matthew, what was going on in his head? We would have to be as patient and tolerant as we could, and hope he would get over his depression soon.

He was no better when his birthday arrived and he asked me if he could postpone it, as he didn't feel like having a celebration.

'We can't postpone birthdays, Matthew. Tomorrow you will be twelve, whatever happens. I tell you what though—we'll have a double treat next year when you are thirteen.'

Poor Matthew, when would he recover and be his old sparkling self again?

My visits to see Mr Wallace continued monthly throughout the year. He was always so delighted with my progress and the way in which the orbit was healing. I would come away from his visits feeling extremely confident.

So confident was I, that I applied for a new driving licence. On the form I wrote down where it stated disabilities—loss of eye. They returned the form with yet another form asking for medical details. I filled them in and sent them off. Two weeks later, a phone call from Dr Perry.

'What's all this about a brain tumour?'

'Oh dear. They had assumed that as I lost an eye because of a tumour in my head, it must have been a brain tumour.'

Eventually, the licence arrived with a little letter: The disability licence is issued for one year only, as it is possible for the condition to recur. Re-apply when necessary.

I flung the bread-board down the garden. I felt better after that.

It is difficult to imagine what effect my illness and problems have had on the children. I only hope it has helped to make them understand that nobody has to have a problem on their own. To share everything, sorrow, joy and happiness is the most important thing in anyone's life.

I discuss everything with Claire, she really is my best friend. Claire says her saddest memory of my illness was when she came to visit me in Wexham Park Hospital, after I had undergone surgery for the maxillectomy, and she had helped me put on a clean nightdress. It was then she saw that the bones in my back and my arms were like a skeleton's. She felt sick.

Dominic remembers the long ride to London and the lift. Best of all was the McDonalds hamburger that we bought for them.

Matthew doesn't talk about it. He simply wants to forget.

Chapter Sixteen

Now we looked forward to the 1980s with new hope. My progress had been remarkable. Mr Wallace told me that I could never be the same as I was, but I was stubborn enough to try. My visits to see him stretched now to three-monthly intervals. In between those times, Claire misplaced a disc in her neck on the trampoline at school. I was visiting Heatherwood Hospital every day, driving myself in my mini. Something I could never have imagined myself doing even three months before.

What would we do without our offspring to keep us busy? As Dr Perry so aptly put it, 'You Piffs don't do things by halves.'

Ken Thomas, a Crowthorne man suffering from terminal cancer, started a Body Scanner Appeal, and my Friday mornings were given to him. I did very simple things like addressing envelopes, having to borrow Ken's father-in-law's magnifying glass so that I could see the telephone directories. I attended school on Mondays for reading, and looked forward to September for some new faces. The children would no doubt ask me the same questions, 'What's the matter with your eye?' and, 'Can you blink?'

It didn't embarrass me any more. I would answer the children honestly and tell them I had cancer and had to have a bionic eye. Life seemed really wonderful. I did the things I wanted to do when I chose to. My whole world was seen once again through rose-coloured spectacles.

It had taken the boys and me all week to prepare the caravan for our summer holiday. I missed Claire's help. It was hard to believe that my little girl had grown up to be such an independent individual. She was spending six weeks with Chris's relations in Canada. I missed her company so much, she had the unique gift of turning every situation into fun. Matthew and Dominic were so excited, they teased each other good-naturedly and bubbled with enthusiasm.

Friday evening arrived, the boys were near bursting point when Chris arrived home. He had bought them a large inflatable dinghy for their holiday. It was immediately inflated on the lawn and the boys sat in it, pretending to row on an imaginary sea.

To our delight, Chris suggested we all went out to dinner: we would start our holiday immediately. I have never seen Matthew or Dominic wash and change so quickly, the transformation was spectacular—if not breathtaking.

I put my arms around Chris and kissed him. 'Thank you darling, this is a lovely idea, and a super start to the holidays.'

The next day was so busy. The boys helped Chris wash the caravan and pack the last few games, chess, draughts and my favourite, snakes and ladders.

'Let's hope we won't need them. It is going to be so hot, we will be sailing the dinghy all the time.'

I was so busy preparing lunch for us all that I almost forgot to clean my orbit. I rushed upstairs whilst the boys played in the garden. What I saw made me freeze inside. Nausea filled my stomach and my heart pounded. On the top of the orbit I saw a small, shiny lump, the size of a grape.

I didn't know what to do. I *couldn't* tell Chris. Panic-stricken, I grabbed my handbag and ran out of the house, hoping the boys wouldn't hear me and follow. Chris was cleaning the fanlight of the caravan on the drive.

'I'm just going to buy a cake, won't be long.'

He looked up and smiled. 'Be careful.'

I drove straight to Dr Perry's home, praying he would be in. Surgery had finished over an hour ago.

Anna, his daughter answered the door. I entered the hall and Brenda, his wife, came out, pulling a top over her head. She had obviously been sunbathing.

'Oh, it's only you, I wouldn't have bothered if I'd known.'

'I don't want to see you, I want to see Dr Perry.' It sounded very rude. Her smile faded, and Dr Perry came out into the hall. He immediately realised there was something wrong and took me into another room. I explained to him what had happened and showed him.

'I'm sorry Christine, you're going to have to postpone your holiday until you have seen Mr Wallace.'

'But Mr Wallace is away. I saw him two weeks ago and he said he was away for all of August.' I fought back the tears.

'Who else have you seen at Wexham?'

'Nobody else. I have only ever seen Mr Wallace.'

'Well you must see someone. Go along on Monday and see his registrar, he will be there. Ring me if you need me, and phone me on Monday evening.'

I left feeling very sick. How was I going to tell Chris and the boys? They would be so disappointed.

I drove to the village and bought a cake. In a silent daze, I prayed I wouldn't meet anyone I knew. I felt so sick. How could I explain to Chris? He was still there on the drive as I pulled up. I carried the cake in my hands, aware of how cold the box was, oblivious of anything else. Here I was again, the same sensations, the same black tragedy of despair filling my body. And there he was smiling and happy. Why, oh why, had this hateful thing appeared today? Today of all days, and now I had to tell him and shatter our lives once again.

'Come indoors, Chris, I want to talk to you.'

'What's the matter?' He followed me into the kitchen and I swallowed hard.

'How would you like to go on holiday on Monday afternoon, instead of tomorrow?'

'Why?'

'Because I have to go and see someone at Wexham Park on Monday morning. I've just been to see John Perry. There's a small growth in my orbit.'

Chris went white, his hands fell to his side and he leaned against the worktop.

'Don't worry, darling, it's probably granulation tissue, but we can't take the chance of going away.'

He put his arms around me and we both tried hard to control our tears.

'Why wait until Monday? We'll go now.'

'I must explain to the boys first.'

The composure took over as quickly as the despair had done and I called the boys in.

'I'm sorry, boys, but I have just been to see Dr Perry as there is some granulation tissue growing in my orbit and he thinks it would be wise for me to see another doctor before we go on holiday.'

They were like two balloons and the air slowly fizzled out of them as they listened to me. Neither of them spoke. Then we phoned Wexham Park and explained our problem to a staff nurse. Kindly she made an appointment for the following day to see Mr Wallace's registrar. I felt ill at ease at seeing anyone else other than Mr Wallace. How would anyone else know what it was—this doctor probably hadn't seen one before. I'd probably end up having to see Professor Harrison. If I had to wait two weeks to see Mr Wallace it might have grown at such a rate it would be too late. All these stupid, selfish thoughts ran through my head. Oh where was Mr Wallace when I needed him so much? I knew I would feel better if I could just talk to him, nobody else understood me as he did.

Next day we were back at Wexham again. The boys insisted on coming and I agreed. They stayed in the car whilst we walked up to Ward Eight.

The registrar was charming, with hands like a pianist. He said there were three small grape-like polyps there, and there was no need to worry. I thanked him and told him he should try sitting in my chair if he thinks I won't worry.

Then he told me, 'It's more than likely granulation tissue, but I think you had better see Mr Wallace. He'll be back tomorrow morning.'

The boys were not happy, but Chris solved this problem, by taking us all to Kew Gardens. It was a warm and sunny afternoon and we had a lovely time. The boys couldn't believe the size of the fish in the lake, and promised to bring some bread next time they came.

Then the same familiar seat, the same door, the same picture of the tiger cub and the grasshopper. Mr Wallace had done his ward round, but was going through all his mail. Heather, bless her, was apologising profusely at keeping us waiting. I felt like breaking the door down. I felt cold and sick! It couldn't be back again, could it?

'Christine, would you come in.'

Mr Wallace examined the orbit and I could see the disappointment on his face.

'Well, Christine, I'm afraid you had better come in on Wednesday and I will take a biopsy under anaesthetic. You should be home on Friday and then you can go away the following week.'

Once more I broke the news to the boys. 'I promise we will go away on Saturday,' I said, determined that we would!

Matthew was reading a book. He looked up at me and said, 'Why is Mr Wallace taking a biopsy?'

'Just to check that the growth is healthy tissue.'

'Could there be any cancer cells in there?'

I swallowed hard. 'Good gracious, I hope not, Matthew,' I said, pretending to be surprised by his reaction. 'But if there is, it would be much better to find out now and remove it, rather than leave it and let it grow.'

Guess what we did on Monday afternoon? We bought two stale loaves and fed the fish at Kew Gardens.

On Tuesday we bought six new fish for our pond. It had been our summer project to build a fish pond. The boys and I had always wanted one but Chris had said that the leaves and pine needles would make it impossible to keep a pond healthy.

Still, we had been out and chosen a large plastic pond. Sadly it was too big to fit in the car, so the owner of the shop promised to deliver it. Unfortunately, he did: later than promised, and Chris had arrived home earlier than usual, so when he saw the man walking up the path with this huge pond the boys were terrified at his reaction.

Chris just looked at me, with one of his superior looks. He would have nothing to do with the pond at all and told me I was mad!

It took us three days to dig a hole big enough for the pond. We hit two tree roots and Matthew and Dominic chopped them with an axe. We felt very proud when it was finished. Then we sieved the soil to pack the sides in. I must admit it was a hard job, but I wouldn't say so to Chris. We filled the pond with plants and I bought one fish each for the boys. The tadpoles and water snails looked so lonely.

As Chris put the new fish into the pond his eyes met mine and we laughed.

'Who didn't want a pond, then?'

'It's a lovely pond, it really looks good.'

'Good. Can we have a waterfall and a fountain next?'

The boys laughed. 'Oh Mummy, you are terrible!'

I looked at the fish swimming about in the pond. If anything happens to me, I thought, the boys will always have the pond and the fish as a lovely memory of our last summer together.

Sleep didn't come easily on Tuesday night. The thought of leaving Chris again made me feel sad. He was distraught, I couldn't cheer him, as I lay in his arms I decided to be honest with him.

'Darling, if it is cancer again, we will have caught it very quickly. After all, I saw Mr Wallace only two weeks ago and it wasn't there then. Anyway, perhaps it will be third time lucky. I recovered the first time and I recovered the second time. And if necessary, I will the third. I have no intention of giving up now.'

I didn't sleep at all on Wednesday night. The day had been filled with the usual routine: blood tests, medicals and signing the consent form. Reuniting friendships with some of the nurses.

I lay there not believing this was happening. The past three years had been hard, and I had fought all the way to survive. I was so grateful for those three years, and never once had I taken a day for granted or wasted a moment.

My gratitude to Mr Wallace was immeasurable. If it was not for his skill and care I would never have had those years. How lucky it was that he was back this week, just when we needed him. He was going on holiday again on Saturday. And I was determined we would be too.

Chapter Seventeen

'It smells in here, Mummy. It smells of hospital and so do you.'

'Well, you smell of pencil sharpeners when you come home from school and I don't complain.'

I was still very drowsy and fought hard to concentrate. Matthew and Dominic were so happy. Chris had taken them to London to keep them occupied and they were bubbling away with excitement.

'Guess where we have been?'

'To Kew Gardens?'

'No, Daddy took us to the Basingstoke canal and we hired a boat for an hour.'

'Matthew couldn't steer it.'

'Daddy couldn't row straight.'

'Who was it who bumped us into the bank?'

I looked at the three of them, recalling their expedition along the canal. They were so funny, not in the least bit concerned that they were visiting me in hospital.

I was nodding off to sleep again as the boys kissed me good night. 'Come and collect me tomorrow, and we will go on holiday on Saturday, promise.'

It was a wonderful week. The sun never stopped shining and the boys lived in the sea with Chris and the dinghy. Chris even persuaded me to lie in it and sunbathe. He had attached a long piece of rope to the end and he and the boys dragged me over the glistening water.

We never mentioned hospital once. We just lived every

minute and crammed our lives so full of fun and pleasure, it was like one long feast.

One sunny afternoon we went mackerel fishing. I was the only woman on the boat. Matthew and I were partners and Matthew caught the first fish, and then Dominic pulled in his catch. It was as if someone up there was looking after us, and making up for the previous week.

When we travelled around in the car, Matthew's hand was always on my shoulder. I don't know if he was trying to reassure me or himself. It was moments like those that let the anxiety creep back.

Early one morning we decided to walk up over the cliff top. It was a long, gradual slope and the boys heaved me over the stiles and took undignified photographs of me as I climbed awkwardly over the bars. I collapsed in a heap on the grass, overlooking the sea. The insects buzzed around and the birds soared high overhead. Dominic and Chris continued on, but Matthew wouldn't leave me.

'Go on, I'll be all right. You walk on with the others.'

'No, I'll stay with you.'

I looked at his silhouette against the sky. He was so young, and yet he understood the agony we were all suffering. By staying with me he was in his way supporting me and showing me how much he cared. I looked up and saw Chris an inch high and Dominic half his size standing on the edge of a cliff, surrounded only by the sky.

'Look, Matthew, look where they are.' He bent down and kissed me, then ran after them.

Over the past years I had accepted that death must come to us all and I wasn't afraid of dying. Indeed my only comfort in dying was that when my new life began I would be whole again. I could smile my old smile and have a complete face and my eye would be there.

Once I dreamed I had died and I was in my new life and I met a man on crutches with only one leg. I shouted at the man, No, no, you can't have died, because you would be whole again. I put my hand to my face and there was the eyepad. I awakened sobbing and so frightened. It's only in my subconscious that I have these doubts and fears. Nearly every night since I lost my eye I have dreamed about it. Perhaps this is the way one copes with traumatic disabilities.

I looked at the three of them now walking away from the cliff's edge. If it is cancer again, I won't give in easily, I'll fight with all the strength I have. I will not be parted from my family.

'Who's for a walk?' It was after nine o'clock and I was tired. But it was our last night before our return home, so the four of us walked through a farmyard, near the caravan. Chris was in front, telling us to be quiet. It was dusk and the birds were making weird, unusual sounds.

We stopped chattering and listened. I found a long pile of telegraph poles lying on the ground, overgrown with grass.

'First to fall off is stupid,' I cried, leaping on to the pile—and promptly falling off. The boys and I had great fun. Chris told us to behave and walk behind each other, as we were now down a country road.

It was nearly dark, and Matthew said, 'This *is* boring.'

'Listen to the night sounds,' I said. 'It's so exciting.' Matthew and Dominic still looked glum. 'Okay. See who can spit the furthest!' The boys thought this was great and proceeded to work up a saliva.

Chris looked at me horrified.

I won't describe the scene that followed, because I can imagine everyone's disgust at my suggestion—especially Mr Wallace!

Needless to say, I dribbled down my chin, falling over with laughter. Dominic kept swallowing his when he laughed. Matthew was pretty good. We had to stop, as a car was coming, and as it passed Chris shouted out, 'I'm the winner!'

'You haven't tried.' yelled Dominic.

'Yes I did, on the car and it's still going. I'm the winner!'

We all chased him down the road.

As we all lay tucked up in our sleeping bags, full of peanuts and crisps and hot chocolate, the boys announced that it was the best holiday they had ever had.

'Good night, boys,' Chris called.

Dominic's voice, much deeper than usual, spoke out. 'Good night God, good night Jesus, good night Mary, good night Joseph.' Short pause; then, in a higher, brighter voice, 'It never costs too much to keep in touch.'

We all laughed so much that the caravan rocked from side to side.

Home. I was sad the week was over and I dreaded the thought of Monday looming so much nearer. Claire was coming home on Friday. I couldn't wait to see her, and hear about her adventures in Canada. How we had all missed her and longed for her return. At the same time, I feared her return in case I had to tell her the sad news. I was torn between the pleasure of seeing her again and the dreaded thought of what Monday might bring.

Sunday was filled with so many chores, every moment was occupied with some activity to keep our minds away from Monday.

My appointment was at 10 am. Matthew kissed me goodbye, Dominic gave me four kisses and said, 'Have a nice day.'

I clung on to his small warm body, finding comfort in his touch.

'You too, darlings, have fun, see you later.'

Chris took my hand, 'Come on, time to go.'

The clinic was crowded. The seats outside Mr Wallace's room were occupied. Chris and I stood up against the wall. Then Chris's hand squeezed mine. 'It can't be that much longer.'

I was the last patient left, and the nurse came out of the door smiling.

As I stood up, my knees trembled. I walked into his room. Mr Wallace's back was towards me, his head bent over. I immediately thought the worst had happened.

His chair spun round, revealing a smiling face.

'Hello, hello, sit down.' I sat down, staring expectantly at him, every sense I had straining to hear what he had to say.

'Good news. You will be pleased to hear everything is fine. It *was* granulation tissue. We tried to phone you and let you know but you must have gone away.'

I don't remember walking out of the hospital. I sat in the car and looked at Chris. I couldn't speak, all the emotion and tension of the past three years flowed from me. I collapsed into a pool of tears that engulfed us both and lasted all the way home.

Six years have now passed since my first visit to Wexham Park Hospital. It seems hard to believe that time can go by so quickly.

Over the past two years I have been visiting Queen Mary's Hospital in Roehampton, London, where Mr Brian Conroy has been making my new bionic parts. It has been gruelling, exasperating, exciting and very, very stimulating. Mr Conroy is a brilliant man in his field. Not only is he talented and blessed with a rare gift but he is also aware of the deep emotional struggle his patients are going through. He has the capacity of being able to fill them with confidence and total trust in what he is doing.

Only when I look at the children do I realise how quickly time passes. Claire is now a young woman, full of life and eager to face the world. I gain satisfaction in sharing her experiences and feel proud that she has coped so well. The past years have given her a special understanding and awareness of people and their needs. She remains my best friend.

Matthew is taller than Chris now, over six foot. His life is full of music (loud mostly) and equally tall friends. They fill the house with their laughter and good humour.

The traumatic shock that he suffered slowly left him. Time reassured him, and my continuous progress has slowly healed the wounds.

Dominic is like a breath of fresh air. The house comes alive when he is there. It is hard to believe that he was only seven when I was so ill. Such a heavy burden for one so young. For Dominic actions speak louder than words. He is thoughtful to all the family and his friends. I will find him in the garage mending someone's puncture or fixing a bicycle.

He doesn't speak of my disabilities as Claire and Matthew do. Yet, when I am about to cross the road or walk up a stairway, Dominic's arm is always around me. He understands.

When I look back on the past years I think, what has cancer

robbed me of? My eye, my teeth, my lip, my speech, the way I look. The saddest loss for me is being robbed of the joy I had in looking after young children. I miss them more than I miss my eye.

But what I have left is much more. I still have the love of Chris and the children. Life, love and friendship—what else matters?

Epilogue

There are no reliable statistics on the number of people who suffer irrevocable damage to their faces. The most common cause of injury is road accidents, but burns and surgery can also be responsible. Today's sophisticated technology can save people who might otherwise have died; like me, they can have their looks rehabilitated by the brilliant techniques of microsurgery and a life-like prosthesis. But after undergoing surgery these patients are often sent from the safe environment of a hospital back into society to pick up their lives again. It is at this point that a whole new set of problems can arise.

However the face is damaged, the pain and distress caused to the unfortunate person is immeasurable. In many cases it has disturbing effects upon the close family circle and friends. Not being able to communicate their feelings to others can cause great distress. This, and not being able to understand why they feel the way they do can cause deep psychological problems. The sensation of isolation and rejection makes one feel completely cut off and alone.

I was fortunate in having such a wonderful husband and family. But what of the other people, who return home from hospital with no one there to help them? As I became aware of the numbers involved, and how privileged my own position had been, I decided that the only way to repay the enormous debt I felt towards the people who had helped me so tirelessly was to try to help others. So, in January 1984, I agreed to be involved in the making of a film for Channel Four television. The film was made for *20/20 Vision* and its aim was to educate and inform the public about the difficult social problems that the facially disfigured have. Whilst making the programme I decided that it would be an excellent time to launch a Support Network, to be called Let's Face It, to enable people to share their experiences and difficulties with someone who really understood. I was enormously helped in this by the Broadcasting Support Services, an educational charity providing a follow-up service for viewers and listeners. They suggested that I produce a leaflet explaining about the Support Network, giving a short synopsis of my medical history and useful organisations to contact. After the television programme, a box number was given, and people were invited to write in for the leaflet.

Two days after the showing of *20/20 Vision*, the producer of *The Russell Harty Show* telephoned to ask if I would appear in the show. I agreed, of course, so, two weeks later, Chris, the children and I were back on television. It was very exciting, and once again, the box number was given.

As a result of this publicity, and articles in local and national newspapers, I received over five hundred and fifty letters. They are from all over the country, from as far apart as Northern Ireland, Scotland, Wales and Cornwall. I was truly amazed—and saddened that such a yawning gap had existed for so long.

I replied to every letter, and I am now trying to form a Network of Supporters all over the country. People like me, who want to discuss their experiences with someone else who knows. It is easy to talk to your doctor, but he really doesn't understand what it is like to live with such an obvious facial deformity.

Mr Brian Conroy, the chief technician, and the team at Queen Mary's Hospital, have been a wonderful support. He has helped and encouraged me, not only in coping with the new prosthesis which I now wear, but also in helping other friends who have written asking for advice. He willingly gives his time to help me encourage these withdrawn people to have prostheses made for them, so that the quality of their lives can be restored to them and they can find their place in society again.

The Support Network continues to expand. New friends write to me every week, wishing to be part of it. When I started this new project I had no idea that I would need funds for paper and postage. My dear friends were there once more. They rallied round and held a Bring and Buy sale at my home. It really was a most exciting day and we raised £200.54p. I opened a new bank account, called Let's Face It. During the village half-marathon, a friend and his two sons ran for Let's Face It and raised £82. People's support and generosity overwhelms me.

My dear friends Mary and Ray couldn't believe that I could possibly write all my letters by hand. I insisted that I could, and I would. Two days after visiting them, a new electric typewriter was delivered to my home. The note with it simply read, 'To Let's Face It. Love, Mary and Ray.' How can anyone fail when there are so many kind friends helping you along? That's what I want our Support Network to be. An extension of those friends, all supporting and encouraging one another.

For further information about the support link for facially handicapped people, Let's Face It, please send a stamped addressed envelope to:

Let's Face It
P O Box 4000, London W3 6XJ
P O Box 4000, Glasgow G12 9JQ
P O Box 4000, Belfast BT2 7FE